TINKER

Elizabeth Snyder Reed

Tinker

Published by Kick a Pebble Enterprises, LLC

This a work of fiction. For the most part names, characters, places, and incidents are the product of the author's imagination or are used fictitiously.

Interior Book Design and Layout by
www.integrativeink.com

ISBN: 978-0-9890497-5-7 (Paperback Edition)

Dedication:

In memory of my father James W. Snyder and my brother John William Snyder, watchmakers, both.

There is a tide in the affairs of men.
Which, taken at the flood, leads on to fortune;
Omitted, all the voyage of their life
Is bound in shallows and in miseries.
On such a full sea we are now afloat,
And we must take the current when it serves,
Or lose our ventures.
William Shakespeare
    —From *Julius Caesar*

All the world's a stage,
And all the men and women merely players;
They have their exists and their entrances;
And one man in his time plays many parts.…..
William Shakespeare
    —from *As You Like It*

To everything there is a season,
a time for every purpose under heaven;
a time to be born, and a time to die;
a time to plant, and a time to pluck what is planted;
a time to kill, and a time to heal;
a time to break down, and a time to build up;
a time to weep, and a time to laugh;
a time to mourn, and a time to dance;
a time to cast away stones, and a time to gather stones;
a time to embrace, and a time to refrain from embracing;
a time to gain, and a time to lose;
a time to keep, and a time to throw away;
a time to tear, and a time to sew;
a time to keep silence, and a time to speak;
a time to love, and a time to hate;
a time of war, and a time of peace.
    —Ecclesiastes 3:1-8

Contents

Part One. The Time of My Life...1

The Cold, Cold Ground 3

Fishing with Calvin 5

With Malice Toward None 19

The War Between the States........................ 25

Reunion in the Grove 29

Time Flows 39

An Age of Invention........................ 49

Part Two. At the Crossroads 73

The Crossroads........................ 75

Things Have Memory........................ 79

Molly and Mister Tinker 93

The Model T 99

Meeting the Wizard........................ 109

Molly and the Way West 121

Postlude........................ 125

Hydraulic Ram Patent Image........................ 127

Music Leaf Turner Patent Image........................ 128

Epilogue: John D. Weaver 129

Part One.

The Time of My Life

The Cold, Cold Ground

I lay in a fallow field. A dense fog covers me. I can't see my hand in front of my face nor the fellow lying next to me. The dry, stiff corn stubble pokes through my clothes. I didn't sleep much all night.

Our bugler, only a kid, was shot dead yesterday. Random thoughts about him streamed through my frantic dreams all night. *His mother will get word of it. He will not live to marry. He'll never have a family. He'll miss his next birthday. It could have been me.* I say a silent prayer for this young soul and for his family's loss. I know that this is the week my heart issues began.

I can no longer feel the gouge of the cornstalks in my back. It's so cold and damp I can't feel anything. I am numb. I hear "Reveille" being played somewhere in the distance by a new bugler. It comes faintly from somewhere in our encampment, but I can't determine from which direction. This is our call to get up, break camp, and march on. I am tired. We all are. I am totally spent, exhausted, and war weary. Somehow I must find the strength to get up and soldier on. I remain still until the bugler finishes.

Somewhere in the darkness, lying not too far from me, I hear a fellow's low, gravelly voice start up. He is singing. His words are "Mine eyes have seen the glory." Another voice joins in, and another, and then another. "Of the coming of the Lord." I hear my own whispered words coming from somewhere deep in my frozen chest. My voice joins in with the others. "He is trampling out the vintage where the grapes of wrath…" The words of the "Battle Hymn of the Republic" surge forth from me, too.

Gradually, shadowy and ghost-like in the dense morning fog, we are able to see one another. Slowly we emerge. We are all on our feet, standing in some unknown farmer's field singing to the Almighty with all our strength and conviction. We are reminding ourselves of what we are fighting for.

As for me, I am praying for His Divine protection.

Fishing with Calvin

We sit on the creek bank fishing. So far, nothing is biting. The bank is so muddy I settle back into the weeds, which are alive with the buzz of insects. A mosquito lights on my bare arm. I smack it and wipe the bloody mess against my pants leg.

Almost at the same time, Calvin slaps the back of his neck and gets up. "I'm *gonna* walk on down the *crick* and take a look. I'll be back." He pulls his line out, carefully clearing the surface, leaving not so much as a ripple. A worm dangles at the end of his hook. He wraps the line around his pole twice and sets off.

I watch him negotiate around the dense undergrowth and vanish. *Good friend, lucky to have him,* I'm thinking. I sit back in the quietude of the morning and brace myself on my elbows. I study the other side of the creek bank, also muddy, but not as bad as this spot. This is a preferred fishing hole for fishermen and kids alike. There is a slight eddy and a deep pool, which is a good place to catch 'em—if they're biting.

A few sunbeams pierce through the low branches of the dense woodlands and hit my face. I shift slightly, secure my pole, and lie back in the grasses. I close my eyes. Perspiration beads up on my forehead. I feel a pounding in my chest, and as I am about to sit up, the shadow of Calvin passes over me.

"Not any better down there?" I inquire, without opening my eyes.

"No. But look at this," says Calvin.

I open one eye. He's standing there holding a good-sized turtle with legs flapping and flailing in mid-air, going nowhere.

"You all right?" he asks.

"Yeah," I reply.

"John, could ya take my bait and dump it in with yours, so I can put this turtle in my bucket? Clara will make some good soup with this." He stashes the turtle away, casts his line lightly back into the water, and sits down about four feet from me.

"Couldn't find a better place?" I ask.

"No, not really. They're not biting."

I grin at him and comment, "Not yet. You mean they are not biting—yet."

"You always were a hopeful kind of guy," Calvin says. He pauses and adds, "Even when we were under fire."

"As I see it, ya need to be hopeful right then. Especially then," I say.

"From my kind of thinking, that's the time you need to duck and cover."

I don't respond. Calvin likes to talk. We sit quietly for a time. Thoughts of the war are still fresh on our minds.

After a while, Calvin says, "Weaver, I'm going to bring my wagon over here next week and get you. I'm *gonna* haul you to the doctor."

"To who?"

"John, a doctor needs to take a look at you."

I wanted to tell him to drop it, that I wasn't up to talking about it right then, but I didn't say anything. I stayed silent.

It happened during the war, and now nearing nineteen years old, I feel worthless. The war disrupted my life and everyone else's. Things are not back to normal. Would they ever be normal again? I ask myself. Most physical work is just too much for me; five minutes of bailing hay or loading a wagon leaves me out of breath with my heart thumping. I don't have a plan for what to do with my life now.

All my troubles started when we were in the trenches in Petersburg. That's when it started. Or maybe it was on the march there. Big thumps in my chest.

It started up one night when Calvin was lying next to me on the ground. I mentioned it to him, and he put his hand on my chest. He felt it thumping, too, and said, "That hain't normal, John!" He insisted I go to the field hospital right then.

I didn't want to go because I saw some of those men at the hospital. I thought it was best to tough it out, stay away from the hospital, but in the end, it got worse, and they hauled me over there anyway. The doctor wanted to discharge me, but I didn't want to leave the regiment. Our company needed every single man we had, and then some. In the end, the colonel said no long marches, running, or lifting, and assigned me to light duty. I made myself useful at the headquarters.

I relive that moment over and over, and I remember the conversation, clearly. The doctor examined me and told me to stay and sleep in his clinic overnight. He said he would check on me the next morning. He did.

The next morning, he called me to his tent. He indicated I should sit down. I did. He started the conversation by saying, "Weaver, I see you just had a birthday last week."

"Yes, sir," I said. "Seventeen."

He smiled kindly and asked, "Did you get any birthday cake?"

I said, "Why no, sir."

Then he said, "Somehow that hardly seems right. I missed mine this year, too."

Then he said, "Weaver, let's get to your issue. For a fellow your age, I don't like what I am hearing in your chest. I'm going to recommend to your captain that he send you home. You're not much use to the cause with your heart out of rhythm like this; it could prove fatal.

"Now I'm thinking, since you're a very young fellow, it could go back into rhythm. I have seen that happen." He shook his head. "Truth is you're no good for the battlefield."

I considered what he said and politely protested. I made a case for why I should stay on with the unit, how I might be useful even though I was not fit for the battlefield or for a march. I did not want to leave my unit.

Calvin was an experienced soldier and was needed on the front lines, but when he could he came by to check on me. More than anyone else he knew my problem.

"John, did ya hear me? I'm coming over next week. There's an old doctor down in the country that should take a look at you."

"Where 'down in the country'?"

"I'm not exactly sure where it is, but it's down *toard* Gettysburg. On that road *toard* Gettysburg. Clara knows about him, and she'll get us directions."

"Clara knows about this? I mean about my condition?" I opened my eyes and looked at him.

"John, someday you'll have wife, and you'll learn that wives know just about everything. If you don't tell them about something, someone else will, or they'll guess, and if'n they guess wrong, a person can get himself in a lot of hot water."

I guess the look on my face was saying I'm not quite believing him.

He seems set on convincing me and keeps right on talking. "Believe me, John, it's best to come right out and tell a wife the whole truth, whatever it is." Then, as if speaking from experience, he adds, "Saves a lot of aggravation."

I mop my face with my handkerchief. I've stopped sweating.

"Feeling better?"

"Yep."

"John," he says firmly and with confidence, "I don't know nothing about what goes on inside of us, and whenever I was at the regimental hospital and had a chance to learn something, I looked 'way and high tailed it out of there. But, you and I both know the condition you have hain't right."

"Calvin, listen here," I said. "I've prayed about this every day and night since it started, and I think it's going to right itself. The colonel said it could. And I believe him. I don't want to worry my mother about it, so don't mention it to her."

The turtle is scratching around in the pail. Calvin thumps on the lid, and the ill-fated creature settles down.

I change the subject. "Calvin, I'm glad Clara let you come out fishing with me. Doesn't she fuss about us being gone fishing all day?"

"Sometimes. But then some other times it seems she and her sister just want me out of the way. Like today. They want me out of the way." He pauses to adjust his line and continues.

"Her sister comes over to help her. It's wash day, you know. So, before I left, I set up the washtubs and put the scrub boards out in the back and filled up the tubs for her. They'll have the clothes washed, dried, off the line, and folded by the time I get back. I'll rinse the tubs, clean 'em up, and put them back."

"Hmmmm, I see."

His eyes look skyward. "After all that rain last night, it turned out to be a good drying day. Nice, clear skies. That's a good thing. She'll have supper ready by the time I get home. Clara's a good woman."

The turtle commences to scratch around, and Calvin thumps the lid again. "And she'll be real happy with this turtle here." Calvin closes his eyes. I hope he might take a nap.

Calvin's farm is over a half hour ride from here. He has a nice size farm and grows enough to sustain his family with some left over to sell at market or barter for things he needs. I didn't know him before the war, and I often think if the only good thing that comes out of the war is me meeting him, well then that was worth it. He's older and has an eight-year-old, several little ones, and another on the way. He often laughs about that and says maybe I should have stayed in the army.

I close my eyes, and I am just about to doze off myself, when he says, "What are you thinking about?"

"I was just wondering if that darkie ever got to Canada? That's what."

"What darkie?" he says.

"Oh, maybe I never mentioned it. Come to think about it. It was before the war, and I didn't know you then."

"What was it?" He is on his elbow looking at me.

"This was before I volunteered. I was probably fifteen. I was outside doing my chores when I came out around the barn and came face to face with a ragamuffin darkie. I think I scared him as much as he scared me. We both stood there frozen in place, not sure what to do next. I took him to be a little older than I was. I figured he must have been hiding in our woods. Thin as

10

a rail, clothes all ragged. I could see he was nearly starved to death. And he wasn't wearing shoes.

"It was almost evening, and I motioned for him to go into the barn, which is where I think he was heading anyway. I went on into the house and told Mother about the fellow. She didn't like the sounds of it and warned me to be cautious; then she heaped up a big tin plate with our supper and handed it to me. I carried it and a jug of fresh milk back to the barn. He had fright in his eyes, but somehow, he made it clear he appreciated the food. He wolfed it down!

"He smelled like a skunk. I brought him some water and soap and a towel to clean up with.

"It was pretty hard to understand him. It didn't seem like he was speaking English. At some point, he realized I wasn't going to hurt him. And, at another point, I figured out he was saying, 'Canada.' He seemed to be telling me he was going to Canada, and he indicated he was following the stars in the night sky for direction. From what I could tell, he had no idea where he was.

"So, Calvin, you asked what I was thinking. That's what I was thinking. And I'm wondering whether he ever got to Canada."

Calvin puzzles over this. "Now that's really somethin'. You never mentioned that before. I hain't never seen any darkies around here."

I continue. "After he wolfed down the whole plate full of food, I could see he was still hungry, so I went back in the house and explained the situation to Mom. She dug around the closet and found a pair of dad's old boots, which she was probably saving for me to grow into. She found an old shirt and heavy sweater. She put some bread and cheese and apples and cookies in a sack, and I carried it all back to the barn along with a blanket.

At first, I thought he had gone because I didn't see him. I called out several times, and after a while, he crept from behind the haystack."

"Weren't ya scared, John?" Calvin asks, curious and concerned.

"No, Cal, I have malice toward none. I stood there while the fellow rooted around in the bag I brought him. He ate some more. Then he took his shirt off, dug a hole with his bare hands, and buried his old shirt. Mind you that," I say.

Calvin seems astonished at what I'm telling him.

"That's not all. He told me, as best as I could make out, that he'd come from Alabama. I can hardly repeat what he said because still to this day it bothers me so much. But, I'll try. I never told my mother or my brother or anyone else about what he said.

"He told me that his father was near death when his father told him to run away. And, to keep running. He said his father died because their master whipped him severely. It wasn't clear to me why he was whipped, but he said that the slave owner told his father to get down on his hands and knees and that his father obeyed; and then that master got on his back, like as if he were on a horse, and rode him all the way up a hill.

"His people were all forced to watch under the threat of the whip, too. From what I understood, when they were finished having their fun, his father had collapsed. He couldn't move and was just lying there on the ground, probably near death. Some other darkies were told to pick him up and carry him back to his cabin. Somehow, he explained to me that his father's knees were skinned and bleeding, his bone was showing right out of his knee, and his fingers and hands were worn off."

"*Lawzy.* That is a terrible story. You know with the war and all, I've seen and heard a lot, but that's the worst thing I ever heard." Calvin is shaking his head in disgust. "I can't imagine a person could be that evil."

I go on. "Mom and I didn't sleep well that night knowing he was in the barn. In the morning, she fixed pancakes and a big breakfast for him. I took it out to him, but he was gone. I often think about him, and I've wondered ever since if he got to Canada or a safe place."

"Let's hope so."

"I can't fathom it and can't hardly abide the thought of that kind of cruelty," I say.

We sit quietly with our thoughts. Then Calvin asks, "Is that why you volunteered?"

"No. Not really."

Calvin didn't say anything for a while, so I ask, "Why did you volunteer, Cal?"

"It's hard to put into words, but basically it was for Clara and my folks. When I enlisted, we had no idea if the war was just starting or it was about to end. They were pushing into the north, and I was afraid they would get into Pennsylvania, and well heck, they did. Heck, Gettysburg is only a good day's march from here.

"My dad didn't want me to go. Clara was pregnant; but Dad and I discussed our way of life, and we both felt the Union and our liberty was something worth fighting for. How we do things here in Pennsylvania seems mighty different than running a farm with slave labor. I couldn't fathom that. My dad, rest his soul, was a thinker. He ventured that maybe if those southern plantation owners were successful at busting up these United States, they might take our land and enslave us, too."

"He said that?"

"Yaw. He would have gone in himself, but he was too old and not well. What about you?"

"It's complicated, but for me, at that time, it boiled down to the legacy of the Revolutionary War. You know my mother and her people were from Philadelphia. My dad immigrated from Prussia, so he had a different life story. Not to say Dad was not patriotic because he was; but, with my mom, patriotism flows through her blood. Her people were in this country already for a generation. Like when they called it Penn's Woods. She felt that if the hooligans from the south were allowed to split this country up, I mean divide it in half, then those who fought for our freedom in the Revolutionary War, including her ancestors, would have died in vain. That's how she put it. Died in vain."

I sit, thinking and choosing my words. Then I say, "So for me, when I volunteered, I was fighting for 'one Nation indivisible.' I guess you could say that for me, emancipation and the abolition of slavery was not the main issue for me, when I went *in*.

"When we were encamped, I listened to the things that were said by the men around the campfire at night. I learned a lot. They opened my eyes. It seems they all had opinions and their reasons for being there, but even today, I'd have to say, I went *in* to protect my family and preserve the union."

Calvin leans forward and checks his fishing line. "I'd have to say that over my years in service to this country, I was beginning to wonder if it would ever come to an end. I saw too many die. Sometimes I wondered if I'd ever get back to Clara and the baby. You know that while I was gone, both my mom and my dad died. I wasn't there for them. I feel bad about that. I feel guilty. A lot fell on Clara while I was gone.

"The war changed me, and in the course of it, I changed my thinking. I walked up and down the Shenandoah Valley so often my boots wore out. And my feet still hurt!"

I smile at him. "I know. You told me that before."

"I know you got stuff that hurts, too.

"John, I've listened to a lot of soldiers and their opinions. I would never call myself an Abolitionist, but I can say I am strongly, very strongly, against slavery. I did my part. I went to fight for my family and our freedom. When I think back on it, I guess I wasn't very smart because when I signed up, I didn't realize I could have lost my life fighting for another person's life."

I think to myself, *It was a noble cause*. But I don't say it out loud.

For a long time, we just sit there watching the creek flow with nothing to say. I sit quietly, thinking random thoughts of things I'd rather forget. Maybe the passage of time will help me forget all that I saw.

Then Calvin breaks the silence. "Do you ever think that just by the coincidence of your birth you may or may not have to fight in a war?"

"What?" I look at him sidewise. "What do you mean?"

"I mean, well for example, right in your own family, your younger brother is two years younger than you. Because of the coincidence of your birth, you served, you went *in*, you were the right age, but he was too young to serve. I was the right age, too, but my dad was too old. The war ended before your brother was old enough to *go in*. It's all about the coincidence of your birth. That's what I think."

"Well, damn, Calvin. I didn't know you were such a deep thinker. You're not going to get all philosophical on me, are you?"

"Phila what?" he asks.

"Forget it," I say. "But, Calvin, you do have a very interesting point there—about the coincidence of birth. I never thought about that before. It never even crossed my mind. It's definitely something to cogitate on."

"Yes, John, think about that."

"What I do think about—since it's over with—is that we may have saved the Union, and we may have emancipated the slaves according to law, but I am not sure this war is over. Not by a long shot."

"Time will tell," Calvin says.

"I think they ought to release all the Johnny rebels from prison. General Grant is right about that. Let 'em go home. I doubt they weren't any smarter about what they were doing and why than I was. Then they ought to hang or imprison their leaders—the generals, colonels, and the majors. They're the ones who wanted to separate the States. They are traitors. Like General Lee. He's the one that gets under my skin," I tell him.

"Yaw," he nods in agreement. "I think you're right. I don't think the government's plans for reconstruction will fix a lot of disgruntled folks. I'm thinking it could be a problem for the generations to come. I hope it gets fixed, so my grandchildren do not have to *go in.*"

"Only time will tell."

"You're right, only time will tell."

My thoughts go to the nights we slept on the cold, wet ground. A shiver runs through me. "Darn, Calvin, some of them soldiers would fly into a rage. 'Member them, Cal?"

Calvin replies, "Yaw. Remember that red-headed fella from New Jersey? His face would get all red when he'd get hot under the collar about something another fella said or did. Seems he was always looking to pick a fight about something with somebody. My guess is that he needed a reason to blow off some steam.

16

"I don't know how, at the end of the day, those fellas had anything left in them to fuss and argue over slave holding and all the finer points of the war. More than once in the mess tent that fella from New Jersey got into it with another *Johnny*; and the sergeant had to step in before they got into a fistfight.

"One time, it started after some negro hunters showed up in camp looking for a couple runaways. 'Member that?"

Calvin went on, not waiting for a reply. "The colonel wasn't in any way hospitable to 'em, and he ran 'em off; but that night, one fella from New York made a pretty strong case for why they shoulda been shot. Every soldier had a different opinion."

In disbelief of his own thoughts, Calvin shakes his head back and forth. Then goes on.

"Do you remember the fella who didn't think the negro runaway that helped cook in the mess tent should have been there?"

I say, "I don't remember that. I'm not sure I was with your Company at the time. But what I do know for sure is that I am changed forever. My heart is changed because of that war."

"Maybe you just grew up."

I don't reply. The creek flows along in silence. We watch.

Calvin checks his pocket watch.

"About the heart thing, John. Maybe this doctor can help," Calvin ventures again, as he pulls up on his fishing pole and wraps the line around it.

"Let's pack up, John. This turtle awaits his future."

With Malice Toward None

Today is a splendid day. The sky is crystal clear, and the cool spring gives way to a pleasant warmth. We are in the wagon bouncing along, with Calvin doing his best to avoid ruts and me hanging on for dear life, when out of the blue Calvin says, "John, do you remember when we were fishing and we were talking about why we went *in*, and you told me about that fella' in your barn?"

"Yeah, I remember that conversation."

"Well, you said you weren't *a feared* of him."

"Right. That's true."

"Well, John, I've been thinkin' about this. You said you weren't *a feared* of him because of you had no malice *'tords* any man. That's what you said."

Calvin pauses as he negotiates several gapping wagon wheel ruts. When he gets the horse and wagon back on a steady course, and the normal clip-clop rhythm is recovered, he asks, "What does that mean, John?"

"Well, at the time, I mean, at that point in my life, I had no malice toward any man. I was young—fourteen or fifteen, you know."

"What? What does that mean?"

"It means that before the war, I was of that mind. That was my thinking. I had malice toward no man. After the war, I was changed. So maybe I'd have to think about that some more. You know, rethink how I felt then and how I feel now."

We ride along in silence except for the plodding sound of the horses' hoofs.

"You see, before, actually since, actually I still believe. I mean I still want to have malice toward no man. It's a learned thing. Think about it like lying. You know people learn to lie—so they do."

"I'm confused," Calvin says. "What has lying got to do with it?"

"Nothing directly; except that at the time, I was young, and I thought that having *malice toward none* was a natural thing, and now I think it is a learned thing. It was my dad who used that phrase quite often—kinda like he was reminding himself to have malice toward no one."

Sometimes, Calvin's seemingly endless questions brings me to my wit's end. He is a good friend and always well-meaning, but today, I wish he would be quiet. It being so splendid a day. The air circulates around me in an invisible, gentle swirl.

I really don't want to talk. I want to enjoy the day and think. This is the sort of day where creative thoughts blow through my mind so rapidly, that, try as I might, I can't catch them all.

I watch a young girl struggling. She and her mother are off in the distance carrying heavy water buckets to the cattle. They draw them at the pump, then empty them one after the other into the shallow watering trough. They wear matching bonnets and aprons. My thought is *There has got to be a better way*, or is it something about *Laboring from sun up 'til sun down.* Yes, *There has got to be a better way* getting that water out there. My thoughts come too fast—I can't catch them.

Calvin cocks his head, waiting, looking at me in anticipation. Unknowingly, he crushes the moment, stills my thoughts, and shakes the pleasantry out of the moment. The day is perfect, the weather enjoyable. I inhale deeply. The sooner I put my mind to answering his questions, the better for both of us.

"Calvin," I say, as I conjure my answer, "the army changed me. When you think about it, I mean the experience, not anybody who went through it could remain unchanged. I can only speak for myself. You and I have talked about all this often. But in regard to the *malice toward none,* I'll just say that I observed a lot of men who served in our Company and other men from all over the Northeast and some from the South of this country. If I wanted to take the time, I'd make a study of all the differences.

"You know, folks from around these parts are of a certain mind, mostly. I'm not saying that all men from Pennsylvania think the same, or that all those from New Jersey or Connecticut think the same. But, over time, I've noticed similarities and differences from one area of the country to another. I don't understand it, and I'm hard pressed to define it. Maybe it is something about how they conduct themselves, their demeanor, or their attitude.

"I think it's peculiar that some men I met had malice toward me—and they didn't even know me. I've cogitated on that for a long time since. I considered that maybe some people are just born nasty or mean. Did they learn 'meanness,' or maybe they were born having malice for others.

"I don't know if I figured out the answer or not; but I think it boils down to this: they didn't have a good mother like we did. Or a firm hand to guide them. I think it's just that simple. They didn't have anybody to teach them how to treat others."

"I don't get it, John."

"Ah, shucks, Calvin. You remember when we were talking about telling a lie? It's the same as that. When I was a little kid and told my mother a fib, she knew it right away. Probably I had guilt writ all over my face. If I denied I was telling a fib, she'd never let me get away with it—never, not once. She'd looked at me straight in the eyes and ask, 'John, are you telling me a story?' Sometimes I continued with the fib, and then it went from bad to worse. If I didn't admit my bad deed or my fib, she'd say, 'Well, John, you just sit right up here on this here chair until you remember what happened.' She'd rather hastily grab a chair, move it around in a huff, and put it next to the stove. I'd sit there and she'd go about her chores. It wasn't too long before I came to my senses and admitted not only what I did but also that I told her a fib.

"My brother Henry was bullheaded. He could sit there squirming around for the better part of the day. When our dad came home, he admitted it all right. There was no way you could get away with fibbing or lying in our house. And I would say, that is true of about every household we rode past today."

22

"What does that have to do with *malice*?" Calvin asked impatiently.

"Calvin, it's the same principle. Learned from childhood from my mother and this was reinforced by my father. I think some of those men I met in the army didn't have firm guidance growing up, and maybe they grew up without one or more of their parents. My folks held me accountable for my words and actions; as did yours. It's about learning right from wrong, and that's part of knowing how to treat your fellow man. You don't mistreat people. And you don't have any hard feelings. It is taught in school and in Sunday School, too. Little kids can be mean and even cruel to one another, if allowed. If I was caught being mean to someone, there were repercussions.

"So, as I was saying, in those years, when I met that darkie in the barn, I had malice toward no man. Therefore, I had no malice toward him. That's how I felt then."

"So, you think that after the war you're different?" he asks.

"Let's just say the war and those we interacted with left me with a lot to think about."

"You're darn right about that, John. Me, too."

For the moment, we lapse into silence.

"I want to get off this subject, Calvin. It's too nice a day to be thinking these troublesome thoughts. Let me leave you with something to ponder. We, you and me, grew up among good neighbors with good parents who taught us right from wrong. What if we grew up in a situation like the darkie in our barn did? Who saw his father and others being treated cruelly, who then saw his father suffer and die in front of his eyes, and who ran for days bare footed. Would I be a different person? Would I be left with malice in my heart? I think I would.

"For sure the army changed me, but maybe I changed that day in the barn. Maybe that stranger gave me something to think about. Maybe I learned something from a runaway that was far from my understanding then and still is today. Maybe being confronted with him in the barn that day has given me something to think about that I didn't know or understand then. And maybe never will. Even today I think about him and his plight."

I hear Calvin say quietly under his breath, "If that happened to me, I think I'd have malice *toard* all people. I think I'd have gone berserk."

The War Between the States

I am somewhere north of Petersburg. It's been a long march today, and there was a charge—many are shot dead. I carry on, although what I am seeing has me nearly scared to death. Except for the bugler, I am the youngest in the Company. I am nearly exhausted. We all hope we are nearing the end of the War Between the States. But no one knows. Pretty much all who are left to fight are younger men.

The older ones went *in* first and so are now either mortally wounded, dead and buried, or maimed and back home. A fleeting thought that I might not live to see my mother again crosses my mind. That thought and worse returns again, as I help haul two fellows with shot off legs to the hospital. There, I listen to their screams and cursing and see limbs, arms, hands, legs, and feet in a heap. I also see rows of dead. I turn away.

Please God, I pray, don't let that be my end. My prayer is answered in that I keep my limbs, but I dare say no one leaves the battlefield unscathed, no matter which side you fight on. If only the torment after a night of haunting images of one's best friend bleeding to death and being powerless to help. Or the shock of standing alongside a fellow soldier shot dead right next to you. Being so close to death week after week stays in your thoughts, so that years later one ponders, *Could that shot have been meant for me?*

Vivid in my memory is the night Calvin Henderson and I lay on the ground somewhere in the Virginia woods. My heart started racing and my chest started thumping. I'd never felt that before. I could hardly catch my breath.

Years later, Calvin told me he thought I was near being frightened to death from that day of fighting.

I didn't know Calvin when I signed up, but I learned he lived and farmed in the countryside not too many miles down the road from my home. He was older, a married man who kept a lock of his wife's hair and his little girls in his pocket watch.

Laying there next to me, as we were, he leaned over and asked, "What's wrong, John?"

I could hardly speak. He put his hand on my chest. He felt it thumping and said, "Something is wrong. I'm going for the captain."

I told Calvin it would be best not to awaken him. He agreed to that but added that when daylight came, if there's no change, I had to report to the captain.

As morning dawned, he and some others hauled me to the rear to have a doctor look at me. That doctor intended to send me on to the regimental hospital, but I explained to him I had been there and seen what goes on there. I pleaded with him not to send me there. He told me okay, to stay calm, and he would observe me for a few days.

I prayed and prayed, and then when the chaplain came in, together we prayed to the Almighty. Several more days passed, and the heart pounding stopped—mostly. I stayed in the clinic, which was a large tent full of the infirmed. Except for cries and moans, it provided protection from the weather for several days.

The doctor came in and checked my heart several times a day and asked me how I was feeling.

I told him, "Quite a bit better."

He told me I would be released and sent home to recover. That's what he said!

Respectfully, I spoke up and said, "Sir, begging your pardon, I don't want to go home. I want to stay with my unit."

"Weaver," he said, "you're not fit for battle. I don't want to alarm you, Weaver, but you're not even fit for a long march."

I respectfully protested, saying that I came with my unit, and it wasn't right for me to leave them.

He said, "Weaver, you say you feel better. Do you feel able to walk home?" He looked down at my papers. "Hum. Pennsylvania. That's a week, and maybe then some, walking from here on foot, to your home?"

"Well, sir." I hesitated. I guessed from my facial expression he knew what I was thinking.

"I didn't think so. Weaver, if I were to send you back to your unit to fight, I might as well just murder you right here because that is what it would be. You have a heart problem of some sort. My best advice is for you to head home to recover. He looked at his papers again. This war will be won or lost before you are able to go back to the battle field."

"Sir, I don't feel it's right for me to leave. Sir, I don't want to be a *beat*." I begged him not to discharge me.

He paused, then looked at me square in the face. "Tell you what, Weaver, seeing as how you feel about your situation, maybe you could help in the regimental headquarters. They need all the help they can get over there. I'll talk to the commander. How does that sound?"

"That's good, sir. That sounds really good."

"Well then, unless you hear something different from me today, tomorrow morning, first thing, you head over there." He pointed to some tents in the distance.

"I'll let them know you're coming."

He made some notes in his records, then asked, "You read?"

"Yes, sir. My father saw to that," I told him.

"You write?"

"Yes, sir."

"You cipher?"

"Yes, sir."

"Thought so." He made some notes and indicated I could leave.

Reunion in the Grove

They are riding in from all over. Every time someone arrives in their buggy or on horseback, a lot of backslapping and hand shaking commences. Some men come alone, and others have a wagon full of kids. Some have come a long distance and camped overnight at a nearby campground normally used for prayer meetings and the occasional visiting evangelist travelling through these parts. They come with picnic baskets and hampers full of food; everyone is ready and eager to share what they've brought.

Some of the local men have set up the tables and benches in advance. Their women have strung up festive red, white, and blue bunting. They lay out a big spread. There are platters of fried chicken, ham, German bologna, summer sausages, and all kinds of cheeses. All locally made. Sausages and smoked hams are being sliced up, and there is good brown bread to slap it between. There is plenty of home baked bread and rolls. At this time of year, the tomatoes are plentiful, so garden vegetables like cucumbers and peppers are sliced up and plated, too.

There is a rip-roaring fire going, corns *aboiling* and nearly ready for eating. There is another fire pit for roasting ears and still another with hundreds of sizzling sausages and wursts and brats. Barely congealed now are a couple pans of souse, which melts as the day grows warmer. Three tables are laden down with pies and cakes of all types, and every time someone else arrives, more are added. It is, after all, Pennsylvania Dutch Country, and I have my eye on the shoefly pie. Every woman's prize recipe must be represented here; and, for sure, there will be a contest later in the day.

Watermelons waiting to be cut are piled up next to an empty picnic table, for later. Calvin laughs, elbows me in the ribs, and says, "Enough for an army." Then, taking a second thought, he adds, "Where was all this food when we really needed it?"

There are children of all sizes everywhere. Some come from very large families. Little girls carry dolls of all kinds—fancifully dressed ones with porcelain faces and rag dolls of all sorts carefully crafted by a loving family member. Littler ones hug or drag stuffed rabbits and bears that have their ears and faces nearly chewed off. Boys play tag and chase one another. Some bigger boys have clay marbles in their pockets, and an older man helps them clear out a space while another is drawing a circle in the dirt. They'll stay busy with a marble tournament going all day. Other men organize relay races that will keep the kids occupied. Other kids just run around poking, pestering, and making downright nuisances of themselves.

I help Clara, Calvin's wife, bring the food from the wagon and set up their table. His girls are too young to help, and Clara has her hands full with them. Calvin is an affable fellow. I owe him a lot. Outgoing as he is, he makes his way through the crowd with an engaging smile and a tin cup full of home brewed beer. Occasionally he enthusiastically brings someone over to introduce to Clara or me.

Calvin knows a lot of these fellows because he was *in* for longer than I. He was raised not far from my mother's house, but I didn't know him until we served together. Eventually, he comes back with two single guys my age, one with his elderly father. Clara and I make space for them at our table, and they join us.

We have a grand time. One fellow has a banjo; he's a good picker. Three others play fiddles. They get together and work out some pretty decent music. Some girls dance. Some little ones get silly and "act out." Their mothers give them a stern warning or make them sit down.

A regimental soldier in uniform with a bugle shows up, and near the end we prevail upon him to play taps. He is not a bugler who I had known. Not Sonny. Sonny was about my age and came from an upper branch of the Susquehanna; he lost his life in Virginia.

In the afternoon, the commander speaks. He introduces some dignitaries and *the people who made this possible,* as well as the guy whose land we are on, who never served. All of us stand tall, caps in hand, when he calls forth a captain who reads from a list of names of everyone from our unit who died in the fight. Sonny was on the list. The captain also awards medals to two men who had been overlooked earlier.

I feel grateful to be alive, but by the time he finishes reading the list of the dead, I feel even more so. It's true that sometimes my heart beats way too fast, but it is beating, and I am alive. Every morning and every night I pray for a full recovery. Now I pray in earnest for all those men who gave their life for their country and for their wives and children, whose lives are changed forever.

When the ceremony is concluded, the commander leaves. We are left with disturbing thoughts and mostly unpleasant memories. A lot went unsaid. The events and the misery of the war are not discussed in front of the women and children. After a while, the former tempo of the conversations resumes, we eat more, and we get up and mingle.

"What are you doing since you've been home?" I said to the fellow next to me.

"Been farming my daddy's land. He's up in years—hasn't been no darn good since my mama died. Seems he's just waiting to go on to be with her. That's what I think."

"Did you marry?"

"No, not yet, but I got a girl, and we talk about it."

"What are you waiting for?"

"For her dad to say yes. Maybe next year. She's fourteen."

Most have their families with them; for some of them, their wives couldn't come the distance because they have infants at home and their wife is pregnant again.

Calvin calls me aside. "John, you see them three girls over there? Them are Burke's girls. You remember him, George Burke? He's sitting over there with them girls and that's his wife Amelia, sitting there, too. He lives in Northumberland. You 'member him?"

I search through the throng of folks.

He points. "Over there with his wife."

"You mean that older fellow with the long beard? No, I don't know him, Calvin. I don't think I ever saw him before today," I say.

"Oh yeah, you're right. He'd gone back home when you joined the fight. Ya see, he's lame; walks with a stick. You see he's got the stick there, propped against his chair. Yeah, you wouldn't know him. You came *in* later.

"It was during a *charge* in some Virginia woods. It was. Remember it like it was yesterday. We were going over this stack of timbers, and he wrenched his knee right out of the socket. Terrible thing it was. He was in all kind of pain. They carried back to the field hospital, and he mustered out soon after that. They didn't do much for him but put him on the next wagon headed north. They said it wouldn't heal in time for him to go back to the battlefield. He's one of the oldest guys I served with."

"How old do you suppose he was when he joined up?" I ask.

"Too old. He was among the first to volunteer. Remember, the older men went in first. He was long out when you came *in*."

I took notice to an older man who could barely get around and thought for a second. Would I rather change his injuries for my heart condition?

Calvin went silent. We stood there alone for a moment in a crowd. I wondered what he was thinking, but you don't ask a fellow his private thoughts. There are quite a few men there who had lost limbs. It seems to me that they are smiling and enjoying life as much as the next fellow. Probably they're happy just to be here and happy to be alive. Everybody here is thinking about someone they knew who wasn't. Like Sonny.

I hear Calvin say quietly, "That was bad." Like it's something he tries to forget. "That there at Petersburg. Like really,

really bad. Lucky Burke got out alive. Lucky *I* got out alive. Glad you weren't there, John. We might not be standing here talking."

I don't respond. Maybe he wants to talk. Maybe not. I wait.

Then he goes on. "Those older men were not fit to fight. I mean they were good men and all, but it's just that I don't think it was right to take 'em *in*. As I'm getting older, I see that, and I feel it. I have less ability for running and liftin' and, well, less stamina in general. He was too old, and you were too young. I was just the right age. I'm glad Burke got taken out of the fight with only a useless leg. He laid there in agony for a long time. We were under heavy fire, and there was no one to haul him back."

"What do you mean?" I ask.

"I mean we were under siege at that point, and we were fighting for our lives. A lot died there in those woods that day—and night. Burke couldn't walk, and so he just lay there next to those logs a long time. We had to advance, and I didn't see who carted him off. He told me about it later. I told him he missed the worst of it. Because everything got far worse that day, his name could easily have been on that list they read."

He went silent. After a while, I say, "I'm bushed. Let's go sit with Clara and the kids. You've been gallivanting around all day, meeting and greeting. I bet she wants to spend some time with you."

"Naw. She's got her hands full. I'm sure she doesn't."

"I'm bushed. Let's go set down for a spell," I say.

"Weaver, ya hain't done much a nothin', yet."

"Yes, well anyhow, let's go set a spell."

We amble over and visit with the soldier who came with his elderly father. The other fellow is nowhere in sight. Clara spreads a quilt on the ground and puts the baby and the next smallest down for a nap. Then she sits patiently helping their older girl learn to knit.

Calvin doesn't like sitting. I know he agrees to only in consideration of my heart condition, but finally he nudges me and says quietly, "John, are you looking at all at them Burke girls? Come on. I'm going to introduce you to old man Burke, and I want you to take an interest in them girls. You need a wife, and them are three nice looking young women."

"Really, Calvin?"

"Yep, really. Come on." He got to his feet.

I get up, halfway reluctantly, and excuse myself to Miss Clara. The soldier and his father get up, too. They hadn't heard what Cal had said to me, but they come with us. Calvin seems disappointed that they have joined us. It seems he has plans for me.

The Burkes sit together as a family beneath a large maple tree. Protected by the day's intense sun and heat, they are dappled in sunlight and look quite the picture. The girls sit on two quilts they've laid out on the ground. Old man Burke is seated in a rattan chair they must have carted there from home. His two small boys play quietly together with a sack of wooden wagons, horses, and tiny carved sacks and barrels. Mrs. Burke is attentive to her husband but keeps one eye on the boys, all the while fanning herself.

Calvin had introduced himself to the Burke family earlier and remembers each by name. Being the fine gentleman he is, he introduces me to George Burke and his wife, Amelia, then to each of the girls. In the meantime, the other soldier rejoins us. So, Calvin did the introductions again. This time, Burke stood up, leaning on his cane, extends his right hand, and identifies himself as George Pierce Burke.

Old man Burke is explaining to Calvin and the soldier's elderly father things about his large family. He went on about his eleven children, as fathers do. His wife, Amelia, sits in silence and doesn't engage in the conversation, except to nod her head in agreement from time to time or when he says directly to her, "Isn't that right, Amelia?"

At some point, the soldier who has only just rejoined us suggests that we, the Burke girls, and us single men go over and have watermelon. Cal agrees that's a good idea, and as we go off, he and the older folks continue with Burke's discussion.

And that is how I met Sarah Jane Burke.

Of the three, I think she is the finest. She is fair, with red hair and a few tiny freckles across her nose and cheeks.

All three are corseted to narrow waists and wear long black skirts, heavily starched white shirts, and fine black leather laced up boots. Their hair is tucked up under their *straw boaters* with red, white, and blue hat bands. Not many years separate them, and it's impossible to tell who is the eldest. To look at them, it is clear they are sisters.

We six walk over, get some watermelon, and find a place to sit down.

Immediately I took to Sarah Jane. She has a decidedly pleasant disposition. She is prone to laugh out loud when something or someone amuses her, and she is easy to talk to. Wisps of her reddish hair catch the sunlight and lightly float with a stray breeze.

The tall, thinner one I take to be the eldest; she is Alice and has dark hair. She is dour, aloof, and uses her fan a lot. She doesn't speak unless directly asked a question. I get the feeling there is some place else she'd rather be, or maybe she is just not happy to be here in the heat of the day.

The other sister, Esther, smiles pleasantly but seems timid and doesn't contribute much to the conversation. That one has a little dog with her. The dog isn't timid and makes a low growl or snarls if anyone attempts to pet him. Neither have the personality of their sister Sarah.

I realize later, on our way home, that Calvin's idea was a good one. And it's good the other two guys tagged along. Somehow, the three of us gravitated to one or the other of the sisters. I sat next to Sarah Jane, and both of us immediately fell into an easy conversation. We were comfortable with each other—both of us being honest and direct.

At the end of the day, as we all take our leave, I tell her I will come to see her in Northumberland when I can. She says that's a swell idea.

Time Flows

Standing at the edge of the gorge, I firmly hold Bertha's hand. She is the youngest I have with me today. "Do not step too close—stay back from the edge. You, too, Luther," I caution. Alice and Luther take a few steps back.

"Did you see to the bottom?" I ask. "Can you see that little stream way down there, Luther?"

"Yes, Daddy," Luther replies.

"I can't see it," says Alice.

"Okay, well now then. Come here and let me take your hand so you can peer way down in there."

Seeming unimpressed, my son utters, "Not much water down there."

"Yaw," I acknowledge. "Hardly a trickle, today. Well now, Luther, ya know we're in the dry season, but things can change. It's quite different in the rainy season."

Luther looks at me with more of a question than a statement. "Maybe raging?" He looks back into the gorge again. "Pappa, you mean it could be deep with raging water down in there?"

"Oh, yes."

I like to encourage my children to think. So, I often pose a question and wait for their answer. "How long do you think it might have taken for a little stream to cut a channel through the land—a stream that eventually made a very deep gorge like this?"

I look to Luther and Alice and wait for an answer. I can see my question has set their minds to thinking. I can see the wheels *a-turning*. Neither gives me an answer, and I won't press them. I go on.

"I mean, just think about this. Imagine this place without a gorge. Imagine a vast plain all the way from our house and way out yonder. Think about that." I pause to let that sink in, then go on. "That's the way it was at one time. I'll say eons ago. Then, rainwater on the surface of the land eroded this land and started cutting into—"

Luther interrupts by asking, "Do you mean it was a rut, and it cut a ditch?"

"Yes, exactly." I smile and nod to the affirmative.

Luther continues. "Sort of like what happens when a hay wagon cuts a rut into a muddy road? First, it's not much, but it gets bigger and bigger. If there's a lot of rain, the next thing the road's washed out."

"You're exactly right, Luther," I assure him.

"You mean after a while, it got this deep?" Luther's facial expression changes, and he looks back down into the gorge. "Gee whiz!"

"Yes, it took centuries, and centuries more, of course," I say.

The thought of it has piqued his interest and animated him. He leans forward again and takes another look into the chasm. He seems to be looking up and down the walls of the canyon with more curiosity, considering the vegetation growing on the steep embankment.

"Golly. That's really steep. It's too steep and too rough to get down there," he comments.

"There is another way to get down there. When you're a little older, we'll take a hike down there. Would you like that?" I ask.

They each nod their heads enthusiastically, including the well-behaved Bertha, who is nearing four.

Often on Sundays, I take a few of our children out to search for arrowheads or collect rocks. As my father knew before me, there are lessons to be learned beyond school books. It's easy for me to find a reason to go for a walk or a hike. It's a good way to engage the children, and fresh air and being in nature clears my head. Besides, keeping a few of the oldest occupied for a few hours gives their mother a moment to catch her breath. She appreciates that.

Years ago, I found this gorge while searching for a fly-fishing spot with Calvin. It's deep in the wilderness, so pretty rugged, but with a picnic basket and a ride in the wagon, I think the kids like the challenges of the woods, and I find it restorative.

Just for a second, I think about my fishing experiences with Calvin. Pleasant thoughts flash through my mind. I smile as slippery, muddy creek banks come to mind, of fishing all day and catching nothing. Calvin passed quite unexpectantly, recently. My close friend and confidant, gone.

Finished with our "expedition" to the gorge, we go back to the wagon. The oldest takes out the picnic basket and two quilts. Betha and I pick a few leaves for her "collection." Looking around, we all agree to a spot under a nice shade tree. Luther and Alice spread the quilts on the ground and lay out the picnic Sara Jane made for us.

On the way home, the girls fall asleep in the back. Luther and I fall into a conversation to the rhythm of the horse plodding along. We talk about a fall adventure in the woods, with an aim of checking out the bottom of the gorge.

Family and friends. That's everything.

In the words of Henry Wadsworth Longfellow, "There is a beautiful spirit breathing now

Its mellowed richness on the clustered trees, and...."

I'm dreaming, and for the moment, I am standing with my brother and sister reciting the Apostles' Creed. We are drilled each morning by my father. He is a stern taskmaster, and I can recite the Creed in four languages. I never required this of my children.

I feel the refinement and gentleness of my mother, who brought a balance to his firm hand in our family. I consider that I am an amalgam of their qualities.

I feel their spirits waft around me in this moment. Intense thoughts of my mother engulf me, and somewhere in time, I know we will all travel together again.

My dream engages me with the Brown family of Philadelphia, a prominent family. These are grandparents I never met. I was told they lived too far away to visit, but as the story goes, they were extremely dissatisfied with their daughter, my mother, who chose to marry a Prussian immigrant—a person much older than herself.

In my dream state, I see her sitting upright in a ladder back chair in the early morning light, making lace in the manner of Belgium lace makers. Rapidly she throws the small spindles in complicated moves; she is a master of a dying art.

Everything is blurry now. It is as if I struggle to look at my life through a piece of her lace. My rational mind runs rampant and is thinking, *Time has changed the fashion of the day, and there is not much need for lace anymore.* Maybe a little trim on a ladies' dress but certainly none is needed for men in this day and time. Unlike those pictured in art history books—those Dutch, who only a couple generations back populated Penns' woods.

Yaw, lace is now just about as useless as high button shoes are today.

In the words of Henry Wadsworth Longfellow, "The life of a woman is full of woe, Toiling on an on, With breaking heart, and tearful eyes, The secret longings that arise, Which this world never satisfies! Some more, some less, but of the whole Not one quite happy, no not one!"

Darn woman killed herself with work. Gave birth twelve times.

My thoughts harken back over the years. All those years of raising and looking after our children, nursing them, wiping noses, wiping away tears, changing diapers, teaching them to sew and quilt and to crochet lace doilies, sitting up with them all night when they were sick. All that alone would be enough to wear out even a strong woman. She had a good heart and never complained. Busy with chores morning to night. All that washing and scrubbing floors she did; nevertheless, she still put in a vegetable garden every year. Kept up a garden with flowers and all. She loved flowers—'specially peonies.

Strangely, for a second I consider the numbers: how many diapers she hung out and then carefully folded, how many meals she cooked, how many quilts she pieced, and how many oil lamps she cleaned and filled. How many socks do you suppose she darned in her lifetime?

And putting food by for the winter. Such a busy time. A smile comes to my face just thinking of all the jars of jelly and preserves she proudly put up. Making pickles as the cucumbers ripened and canning tomatoes. Banking potatoes and turnips. Making sauerkraut. Drying corn and apples. Enough apple schnitz to snack on all winter long.

Everyone pitching in, working together, doing their part, even the littlest—family, the ties that bind.

When the girls were mostly grown, the boys were out working, and she had a few moments to sit for a spell during the day, she started takin' in boarders. I was downright opposed to this idea, and I still am. I didn't like it one bit. I got hot under the collar about this. Maybe I should have put my foot down. Yes, I should have. It was a foolish idea, but she insisted, saying the bedrooms were just sittin' there empty, and she had to dust them anyhow. I suppose there's truth to that. Well, it was her choice. So, she just kept right on cooking and cleaning.

Yes, I should have put my foot down, but Sara Jane was a strong-willed woman, and I was in the busiest and most productive years of my life. I had steady watch and clock work in those days, and as any good farmer will tell you, *You've gottah make hay while the sun shines.*

I wonder, how many clothes lines did I string up, and how many clothes props did I make for her over the years? How many wash boards did I buy? All those table clothes, sheets, towels, and underclothes hung were out on the line every day—in winter, frozen stiff as a board. Then she heated the iron and ironed it all. The girls' bonnets were always in starched stiff. As were my shirts. My girls made me proud.

Sara did her duty. I did, too. No one ever went to bed in our house on an empty stomach. She never did take a moment to sit down and rock, except when a baby needed nursing. She just dropped over dead one morning while fixing breakfast for them darn boarders.

All our children, they were all good children. Not a shirker in the lot. Not a wastrel. All good and productive citizens today. And all married pretty well, too.

From the poet Henry Wadsworth Longfellow, "The men that woman marry, And why they marry them, will always be A Marvel and a mystery to the world."

No layabout husbands in the family. One in haberdashery, one recently went to work for Alfred Fuller, traveling around from town to town selling brushes door-to-door. We'll see how that works out. One working as a typesetter for the newspaper, which is growing and expanding and hiring more every year. One at the dairy business, making ice cream, and then two in the iron ore industry. Dangerous business, that. Smelting. William, the Welsh husband of my middle daughter, Amelia, was injured when a hot iron bar passed through his leg. He's on a pension now. Darn shame that is.

I awaken, still in somewhat of a dream state. Thoughts of family swirl around.

I'm thinking, *I'll close my eyes, and maybe I'll take a little nap.* I'm thinking about the new generation, my grandchildren. I'm thinking about the antics of those little tots. I smile.

Then, for no reason at all, the direction of my dream thoughts changes. I'm going to the Jersey shore with Sara; my images reflect all the fun Sara and I had before all those children came along. We never missed a chance to go to an amusement park. She loved the bandstand.

Many say that dancing is just an excuse for "public hugging," and I tend to agree with that; but back when Sara Jane and I were courting, she liked to dance. That was before all the children came along. I took her and her girlfriends to amusement parks. There were a lot of parks being opened back then, and there are still many more today.

We had fun in those days, setting off to see and hear a special band the girls heard about. Depending on the location, we took a picnic. Sometimes, we took the train and then rode a streetcar. At the end of the streetcar line, often there was a beer garden. That was the entrance to the amusement park.

Many of these parks had rides, adding new ones every year. Quite thrilling rides. Mostly these parks are built on land owned by power companies. Water resources for electric power, which lends itself to hydraulics for operating roller coasters and other rides—that intrigued me.

We both enjoyed amusement parks and the rides. Maybe for different reasons. I was intrigued by how those rides operated. Sometimes, the fellow operating the ride noticed my interest and took the time to show me how things worked.

Water is power.

I fade in and out of my dream state, now fitful. My random thoughts turned to the darkie who showed up in our barn many years ago. I wonder about him and hope he got to Canada or found a safe place to live. Maybe he, too, has a family of his own now. Like myself, his children would be grown, and some would have children of their own. That would be a good outcome. After all these years, I still think of that fellow—a scared runaway, scarred forever by his father's despicable end at the hands of evil men. I pray silently for him and for his father's soul.

When I *went in*, I simply wanted a peaceful and prosperous nation. One nation. Like my mother's ancestors wanted and fought for in the Revolutionary War. I was young and naïve then. Hardly sixteen years old. I'm a much deeper thinker now. Maybe, hopefully, I've gained some wisdom over time.

As a Christian, I can't abide the thought of slavery—one man owning another. I knew in my heart then, and I know now, that slavery had to be abolished. Sometimes, a man has to make difficult choices; this was one of those times. Upon reflection, I'm glad I stood up for the cause. I am glad I fought to rid slavery from these United States. I hold that a man working in the fields, no matter the color of his skin, whether black or white, deserves to be paid a fair wage for his work.

Calvin and I often talked about this—the major issue of our generation. More than once I explained my reasoning to Calvin like this: there's a lot about a persons' self-worth tied up in that issue; any man—black, white, red, or yellow—must have his dignity. I'm satisfied we did our part.

What we fought for, that is the question Calvin and I discussed a lot after the war. I'd say it came up just about every time we were together, except when our families, the children, and the women were around. And still today it is the overriding question. The war is over and done with—but still.

There are those mortally wounded, killed and dead, their bones withering in their graves; and there are those around who are maimed and crippled. I'm among the fortunate.

As Calvin always said, let's hope that in years to come, the descendants of those freed Negros will appreciate what we fought for and realize that more than 30,000 Yankees from Pennsylvania suffered and died on their behalf.

Only time will tell what the legacy of the War Between the States is, I think.

An Age of Invention

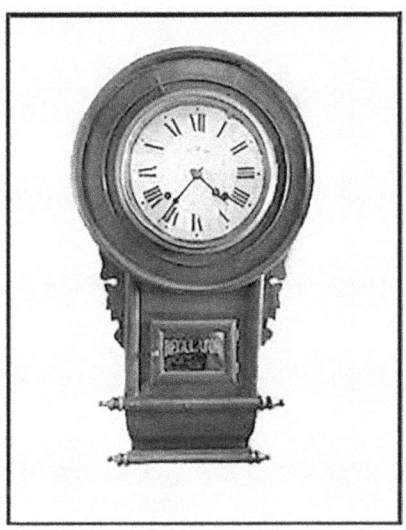

Iam halfway through *The Watchers* when I hear footsteps on the porch. I close the John Greenleaf Whittier's book of poetry I'm reading and hearken. Earlier in the day, I opened the front door to let some fresh air through.

I'm not expecting anyone. Sara hated the pipe smoke in the house. She's gone now, but I carry on her ways. Closing the shades at night to trap the warmth. Opening them in the morning to let the sunshine warm the room. Letting fresh air circulate through on summer days. She had her rituals, good ones, learned in childhood and passed on to our children.

Airing out the house is one of them. We all thrived in her orderly household, and that suited me fine. These days, I try to keep up with everything, but sometimes it gets the better of me. One of my daughters comes by once a week to clean. I'm grateful for that. The girls comment on the pipe smoke, just as did Sara.

"Hello. Hello. John, you there?" I hear his knocking on the screen door frame.

I recognize the voice of Ralph, the husband of one of my middle daughters, Ema. I lay my book aside, get up, and head to the door. "Come on in, Ralph. What are you doing in these parts?"

"Em said wherever I get over this way, I'm to stop in and check on you." He smiles.

I push open the screen door and beckon him in. "Want to come in? Or would you rather sit on the porch?"

His coat is slung over his shoulder, and his sleeves are rolled up to the elbow. He holds his hat in his hand. Ralph carries a little extra weight; his face is red, and his forehead glistens with perspiration.

He says, "Let's sit out here; it's a beautiful day we're having, and there's a real nice breeze here."

I step out with my pipe in my hand. We settle into a chair. He takes the sturdy wicker arm chair, and I take the rocker.

"Am I interrupting something?"

"No, I was just reading and having a smoke."

"What were you reading?"

"Some of Whittier and Longfellow's poems. I finished *Evangeline* this week."

"I thought you read *Evangeline* before. Was it last year, or the year before?"

"Truthfully, Ralph, I've read it many times over the years. I guess you could say, Longfellow is part of my dad's legacy. Dad loved books, all books, but especially poetry. He didn't buy many, but he read whatever he could borrow or get his hands on. He loved Longfellow's work and instilled that love of books in me.

Evangeline is one of Longfellow's best works. Whenever I have the time I read it, again, I do. Interestingly, I've found that every time I read it, I get something else out of it. I guess I should say I get something *more* out of it. It's not the book that changed—the words are the same. It's me that changed. It's my age and my situation in life that's different. I see things in his words that I didn't see when I read it before. Even the descriptions and events conjure something different. Funny that.

"Did you ever read it?"

"No, I'm not much of a reader. But, I notice you often quote Longfellow or some other poet. John, I stay too busy. I'm way too busy. With the job and all. I'm lucky to have the time to read the morning paper and the information the company sends me."

"Well, then. I understand that. And, I do remember. There are some years that are so busy they go by in a blur."

John smacked his hands down and rubbed them back and forth over his legs.

"It's good to see you. You're looking good. What brings you by?"

"I was over here in your territory, and I thought I'd stop in." He takes out his handkerchief and blots his forehead.

"Your yard looks good, John. I love this big shade tree. A chestnut, isn't it?"

"Yes. It's getting huge, pushing up the pavement. There are some kids down the street that love it, too. In the fall, they come over and ask if they can gather the chestnuts. When they do, they come up on the porch, I go find an awl, and help them poke a hole through what they've collected. Then I get them some twine, and they string them up to make a necklace. They have fun with that.

"The next-door neighbor boy comes over and cuts the grass once a week. He does a pretty good job."

Ralph is real pleasant to talk to, an affable fellow. I enjoy his company. Has a big personality but modest. A good chap, a good provider, and father of three of my grandchildren. Sometimes gregarious. He's what you would call a "go getter." He needs those qualities to succeed in his line of work. Sales.

A few years ago, he was hired by the Fuller Brush Company. Another of my son's-in-law told me that in just a few years they have expanded his territory, and now he has two sales-men working for him.

Alfred Fuller's company, out of Harford, Connecticut, was established in 1906 and is doing very well. Thriving you could say. Fuller's concept of selling door-to-door is new. He sells various types of brushes, mops, and scrub brushes. Ralph is perfect for that sort of job.

"How are things going for you and the family? How's the new job going?" I pick up my pipe, take a pull on it, only to realize that it has gone out. I lay it aside.

Ralph leans back, looks around, comments on the quiet-ness of the neighborhood, and admires the shade of the huge chestnut tree, again. He has his hat on his lap. He seems to have something in particular on his mind.

"Nice hat. Looks new," I comment.

"It is. I really like it. Good quality felt work." He held it out, and together we admire it. "It's from that new hat factory that started up. They're going great guns. Shipping all over the country. Hiring, too. They've got a night shift, even. They work around the clock. I think they're making some good-looking hats." He admires it again.

"A lot of new mills and new factories in the last twenty-five years," I comment. "A lot of changes."

"The iron ore business and the steel mill are going full blast day and night, too. They're always hiring," Ralph adds.

"Yep. I've seen a lot of changes over recent years. New businesses starting up, and some have gone away. One hardly needs a wainwright anymore."

My new Ford is parked by the side of the house. Ralph looks at it admiringly.

"I saw an article in the *Daily News* about you last week," Ralph comments.

I nod my head to the affirmative. "A young fellow came by here last month. An inquisitive fellow. He wanted to talk about my patents. Not so much about what the hydraulic ram did or the mechanics of the music leaf turner, more like why and how a person goes about getting a patent. I showed him the models and the patents for both items. We sat in the front room for a piece. He read the patents thoroughly, with a keen interest. We had a nice talk. He noticed the clock I'd built and admired it. I told him, that's the clock that was shown at the World's Fair. That got him interested in why I invented the music leaf turner and the ram."

"Why did you?" Ralph asks.

"As I told the reporter, it's mostly about seeing a problem and wanting to solve it. Sometimes a simple device can improve things a great deal. Like, if you're playing a violin, like

I was, your hands are full with a violin and a bow—who is to turn the page? Should I stop playing the violin or the piano to turn the page? Or have a friend turn the page?

"She's been gone a while, so maybe you never met her, but Amelia's mother-in-law was an immigrant from Whales. She was a gifted Welsh opera singer. Her name was Ann Cook. She sang with the *gyamanfa*."

"No, I never met her, but Will mentions her from time to time." Ralph nods his head. "What's the *gyamanfa*?"

"I'd say it's a tradition the Welsh carried with them when they immigrated from Wales. The Welsh are famous for their voices. It's a gathering together for the purpose of singing sacred music, hymns. Like a festival. She sang with the group.

"William was a little fellow at the time she was traveling around the countryside, and what's been told to me is that every time his mother went off to sing at one opera house or another, the little fellow ran away. It must have been hard on him having her gone.

"You know Ann's people came here and established the Welsh Congregationalist Church in Danville and up around Renova. Ministers on that side of Amelia's family. It's really quite something when you think about it; Ann Cook sang for Queen Victoria. Will's mother had quite the voice. People referred to Ann as the Jenny Lind of America.

"Do you know of Jenny Lind? The Swedish-born opera singer? She was called the Swedish Nightingale."

"I've heard of her, but opera is not something I know much about," Ralph acknowledges.

"Ann and I talked about the page turning problem, and I'd say that conversation, plus my own experience, could have motivated me to work on a design to solve that problem. To me, it was a problem that was just asking to be solved. So, I worked on it.

"I have a letter in the front room there, from someone in Europe, who saw the registration for the patent, and they'd like to patent it over there.

"But in the case of the ram, well, I have always had an interest in hydraulics—still do. Water power, now that's the thing!

"Maybe I watched too many women and little kids carrying water by the bucket full to cattle in the fields. It seemed to me there might be a way to pump water out there. There were other rams being developed, but I hope mine improved things even more.

"You know, Ralph, it took me a lot of work to get it right. I found many ways *not* to do it.

"Yes, Ralph, I always had an interest in hydraulics. The power of water! The power of steam! Since I was a kid. Still do. As a little kid, I was always getting scolded or punished for playing in the water.

"I was thinking the other day that these electrical lines they are stringing all over town are really changing things. They're doing a lot of hiring, too. More jobs. People need 'em. The electric power company is putting up poles, way out in the country. They'll be getting electricity out there, too."

Ralph didn't seem really all that interested in what I was telling him. I went on anyway. Seems to me these young fellows don't seem to see what's going on right under their noses.

"You know, it's a lot like Elisha Oatis. He was a genius. There was steam and hydraulic ways to lift a platform before he invented the Oatis elevator in the 1850s. I'm sure he found a lot of ways not to do it, also, but in the end look what he did for us! Reduced all that backbreaking lifting, hauling, and lugging stuff up and down stairs. A vast improvement. Made life easier for many a worker. Lightened the load for many.

"Now his lifts are being installed everywhere, even the Eiffel Tower. They've got them in New York City department stores; someday, I'd like to get into Wanamaker's department store in Philadelphia. I'd stop on all floors.

"Speaking of sales, Ralph. John Wanamaker had this idea to make a one stop shopping place, and we got department stores. Pretty much ended your traditional dry-goods store. Now, this fellow, Fuller, has the idea of selling door-to-door. That's another change. An improvement. People seem to need more things. Things that improve their lives, make things easier."

Ralph immediately responds. "I hear a lot, and I see a lot being in this door-to-door business."

"I'm sure you do!" I raise an eyebrow.

Ralph says, "I heard last week that Huffman's dairy is expanding. He bought out Forrester's dairy last year, and now their buying out the Kelly farms. Hiring, too."

"Well now, there's a business that's changed." I smile. "Are you young enough to remember how the milk man came by on his horse drawn cart with a metal barrel full of milk? All day long the women would be on the lookout for him. Maybe I should say they had an ear out. They had to listen out for him. There was a bell on the cart, and when they heard him coming, they would carry their containers out to the street and he would fill them.

"My momma used to send us outside to watch out for him and run back in to tell her when he was coming. Do you remember that?"

"Not really. No, I don't remember that. A little before my time," Ralph says, scratching his head.

"I can't remember exactly when it was, but whenever it was that they patented the glass milk bottle, well, that changed everything for the dairy business. I've seen a lot of changes over the years, Ralph. That's a really big one.

"You're too young to notice much of it now, but time flows along, and when you get to my age, you can look back and see the changes very clearly. I don't expect to live long enough to see it, but I expect that that insulated milk box sitting right there behind your chair will become as unnecessary as a shoe button hook."

He looks at me, shocked. "Ya' do? Really?"

"I was thinking the other day about throwing away a shoe button hook that Sara had—and used every day when we were first married. The girls, too, with all them high button shoes I bought and paid for. Then I decided against it. It has a nice ivory handle on it. But it's useless. I stuck it back in the drawer.

"Big business, now—shoe laces."

I reach for my pipe, then realize it is still out. Taking both arms off the rocker, I push myself up. "I'm going to have to go in and light this pipe. Could I bring you a glass of water? Or something to eat? Sorry, I should have asked before we sat down."

"Water would be good, John. Shall I come with you?" he asks.

"No, you sit still. You've been working all day. I'll be right back."

When I return, Ralph mentions again how much he likes my front yard, admiring my shingle house and the wide veranda.

"Well," I say. "It's just too much for me. I just rattle around in there all by myself. It's a lot to keep up. Lucky for me, Bertie comes over once a week and straightens things up.

"I'm thinking about moving down in the country. I found something that suits me. Small, quiet, in the woods, a way from all the hustle and bustle and distractions of town living. It's enough space for my books, my work bench, and my easy chair. That's about all I need, now. As I said, things are a changing. And, Ralph, the truth of it is, a person's needs are less the older they get.

"At one time, this was a busy household; but life and things have slowed down. I have, too. I don't need this big place, all this space, and all this furniture. I just rattle around in there. A table, a bed, my bookcase, my easy chair, that's about it. The basics.

"It's a small place. It's in the woods. It's got water and indoor plumbing. All on one level. Ralph, my knees can't take these stairs much longer. I've got relatives that farm over there. My brother Henry's daughter and her family live just up the road.

"The town is too busy and growing all the time. I'm looking forward to getting back to country-living, a slower pace."

"Are you sure?"

"I'm sure a little watch work will follow me out there. Folks always find me when their clock stops. It'll keep me just a little busy. But not too busy."

"Did you tell Em this?"

"Not yet. I mentioned it to Nell. So, Em may know. You know how fast word gets around among my girls.

"A stream runs next to it, and I'm going to build a water wheel. I have plans."

"What?"

"The place I bought."

"Oh, yeah, a water wheel? You're planning to build a water wheel?" questions Ralph.

"Yep, I been working on the designs off and on for a long time. I just need to make time and do it."

I tap my pipe over the porch rail into the forsythia bush, no longer in bloom. Then set about filling it.

"So, tell me about how the new job is going."

"Not so new, John. I've been at it for over two years now," he says.

"Seems only yesterday you started with them."

"I was the first around here. I really like it. I mean going door-to-door. Not so pleasant in winter weather, but for the most part, I can't complain."

"I hear Fuller is going gangbusters all over New Jersey and Pennsylvania. Is that because of your hard work?"

"Well, John, we've got good products. That's the thing! Not only hair brushes that the ladies like but bottle brushes and scrub brushes. Good ones. Good quality bristles. And you know we guarantee them for life? That's a big selling point. I've only had to replace three, and that wasn't because of the brush. It was because of the person's carelessness. A dog chewed up the handle on one. But I replaced it anyhow. Better to replace them than have an unsatisfied customer who gossips. One customer could ruin my reputation."

"I can see where that's smart."

"Last year they expanded my territory and asked me to hire on two more salesmen."

"That's great, Ralph. I hope you got a big pay raise," I say. "I mean with the increased responsibility and all."

"I do good, John. I can't complain about the money. The thing is, John, I wanted to talk to you about something. To see what you think."

"Yes?" I look at him directly as I draw on my pipe.

"I've come to the conclusion that there are some things you can teach a man but some you can't. Some just don't have it. I mean, if a person is the timid sort, they have a lot to overcome just knocking on a stranger's door." He pauses and shakes his head.

"I mean, I can tell them what to say, and even how to say it to the customer, but, John…"

He looks at me as though he wants me to confirm that what he is saying has credence.

I say, "Yes, I can see what you mean. For most, knocking on a stranger's door would be daunting. I don't know that I could do what you do, day in and day out."

He didn't respond, so I went on. "You're a natural born salesman, Ralph."

"A what?"

"You're an out-going type of guy. You always have been. Easy to make friends. I'm thinking you are a perfect fit for the Fuller Brush Company. A natural born salesman. The way I see it, you're a natural for that job."

"Hmmm. I've been trying to work with these two guys. I want them to do well."

He leans forward toward me and half whispers in a somewhat conspiratorial manner. "You know, I get a small commission on everything they sell, too."

"Well, I'll be darned, Ralph. That's a good thing! A really good thing!"

Ralph rambles on talking about the fellows he has not been too successfully training in sales.

I have my eyes focused on the "Fogle and Sons" ice truck, which just came around the corner and is now working its way down our street. One after the other, my neighbors get their ice delivery from the new truck with the Fogle family name hand-painted fancily with scrolls and flourishes on it. Finally, at my curbside, William Fogle's son, Carl grabs his ice tongs, takes hold of a block of ice, and heaves it up on his rug-covered shoulder. He adjusts it somewhat; and then, moving quickly, he comes along the side of the house and heads straight for my back door.

As he passes the porch, I call out, "It's open, Carl."

Under the weight of the ice and the cold, wet load, he grunts, "Ahun."

I hear the screen door slam as he enters the kitchen and then again when he comes out, having put the block in the ice box. Soon he passes by the front porch. "Carl, did you find your money under the mat?" I call out.

"Yes, I did. Thank you, Mr. Weaver, 'preciate it."

"Nice day we're having, Carl," I say.

"Sure is." He waves as he continues on to his delivery next door.

"Nice boys. William's sons," I comment to Ralph.

"Do you know them? I mean the Fogle's," Ralph asks.

"Oh, yes. I remember when those boys came into this world. I knew William. The Fogle Ice Plant was one of my first accounts," I say.

"How so?"

"Well, I knew Billy when we were young men, and neither he nor his wife were good with numbers. His father, old man Carl, set up the plant and got Billy, his only son, involved. They knew ice making and maintaining the equipment and were good at that, but they kept their notes and receipts in about nine different cigar boxes. They didn't have a clue what was coming in or going out. After Billy's dad died, he had a mess keeping up with things. He asked me to help him sort things out."

"Is that how you got into accounting?" Ralph inquires.

"I suppose so. Yes. When I was young, my father, and my mother, too, saw to it that we all could read and write and knew our numbers and could cypher. My dad was a strict taskmaster. Probably I told this to you before, but every morning he lined us up and we recited The Apostles Creed in unison.

"Even through my dad immigrated here from Prussia, he spoke English fluently. Dad was a learned man—a studious sort of man, who appreciated music and poetry and spoke five languages. He was a watch and clockmaker. He built clocks. He taught me those skills earlier on, and I expected to follow him into that business; but he had the idea I should be a shoemaker. His reasoning was that everyone always needs shoes and shoes repaired. He sent me to work under a man in that trade.

"Shoe repair was not something I particularly liked. In fact, I didn't like it. At all. I didn't like the smell for one thing. I especially didn't like how it stained my fingers. Clockwork suited me.

"Dad thought there were enough clockmakers in these parts, and there still is stout competition. He did his best to steer me away from his business. He harped on the fact that shoes always need to be re-soled and heeled.

"Then along came the War Between the States, and that interrupted everything—for me and for a lot of people. But that's long ago."

Ralph, forgetting his problem for the minute, asks, "So, how did you get into accounting?"

"I suppose I just sort of fell into it. Saw a need and filled it. It was after the war and after my father passed on. I knew his trade because, as a kid, I often went with him to someone's house to fix their clock. I could make parts. He taught me that.

"Mom kept his workbench and tools after he passed. After the war between the States, I dropped the shoemaking idea. Dad was gone, and I was dealing with a heart ailment.

"As often happened in those years, people, not knowing Dad had passed on, would come by the house with their pocket watch or with a clock that had stopped. With Dad gone, Mother asked me to take a look at their problem. Mostly I could fix it.

"But about the accounting, one thing led to another. When I was at someone's house about their broken grandfather clock, sometimes folks, knowing I could read and write, would ask me to read a letter for them; or they would ask if I could read or explain a tax notification or read a document to them. When they paid me for the clock work, they added a little more. They appreciated how I helped them out. Sometimes they only read and wrote German.

"You know how word travels; and word soon passed around these parts, so much so that people I didn't even know contacted me. One account at a time I built that business.

"Eventually, I found myself at Dad's workbench every day, the accounting and bookwork business only a sideline. Clock repair is a good business. Steady. There's always a watch or clock needing to be cleaned; always a carelessly handled dropped watch needing repair.

"I was already established with my own shop when Sara and I went to housekeeping," I added.

I look at Ralph, who seems to be considering his next question.

"I know you know this, Ralph, but it's worth saying: reputation is very important. Just as important as what skills you have."

Ralph nods his head in the affirmative.

I go on. "It wasn't long until I had a lot of mouths to feed."

"I know about those mouths to feed," he says, and we both laugh.

"Ralph, you have the five of you. Sara and I had twelve children—actually, fourteen. We lost two in infancy."

"John, I know you haven't worked in sales like I do. I mean door-to-door. But you have, what I'd say, 'sold yourself' pretty *durn* successfully. I mean inventing that hydraulic ram and getting it installed around here. So, you are in sales. And you have accounts."

"My brother's always done most of the installing; he hires some men to dig the ditches and lay pipe."

"Well, John, what I've been thinking about is that if you are a salesman, you've got to get up every morning and you've got to have a goal. That's the main thing—a goal."

He says the word "goal" firmly and emphatically. It seems Ralph is intent on discussing his sales experience and the difficulties with the new salesmen. I nod my head in the affirmative.

He goes on. "I mean you can't be vague about it. Saying something to yourself like, 'I am going to sell brushes today.' But that won't do. It's not enough. It's my thought that you have to say to yourself, 'I am going to sell twenty units today.' I mean, something specific. A specific number. Of a specific item."

"I see what you mean, Ralph."

Ralph goes on. "If you haven't laid down a specific goal, a very specific one, you'll never meet it."

I am cogitating on what he's saying. He makes a valid point.

"I mean, I'm not saying there is anything wrong with a person falling short for the day. Like missing your goal, once in a while. I'm just saying that unless you have a set goal, you can never attain success in sales."

He seems to have concluded with his explanation, so I say, "I see what you mean."

"But do you agree with me? Am I wrong about this? Because these two new guys just don't seem to get it."

Ralph settles back in his chair with a sigh of exasperation, as if to say, *I've struggled with this, and I am at my wits end.*

"Ralph, the way I see it. Well, two things. First, you are what I call a natural born salesman. You've got the gift of gab. You're friendly and outgoing. It's easy for you to talk, even to a stranger. That's kinda rare. Think about it."

"I have," he replies.

"I mean, Ralph, you've got a gift."

He looks at me quizzically. I go on.

"Then secondly, Ralph. Teaching others sales is something altogether different than doing it yourself. Your idea about setting a goal is a good one. Actually, it is well beyond good. It's great. You're successful because you *do* set a goal, and that consistently rewards you. Ralph, that principle can be taught, but I'm sorry to say not all fellows can be successful in sales."

I take a puff and reflect.

Ralph looks tired, like he has a lot to deal with. I go on.

"Some of the problem is their personality, and their inclination, and being suited for the job. This applies to any job you can think of. Ralph, some jobs require a lot of muscle. If you haven't got muscle, don't apply. Others require brain power. Your job requires some of both, plus an extra dose of personality."

Something pricks my memory. "I guess I'll sound like a really old man, which I am, but there was a time when I was a kid, a young man had a choice between being a farmer and being a farmer. That was just about it. When I think back over the years, since the war, so much has changed. There are so many opportunities, choices for a young man.

"Look at you. Who had an idea of selling hair brushes and scrub brushes door-to-door in 1880? Nobody, that's who. Ralph, I can remember a fellow who came by our house once or twice a year with his horse drawn wagon. My mother would look over everything he was hauling, maybe buy something, tea or something, or get her knives sharpened. He sharpened knives. He always gave me a cherry candy.

"No, I can see you don't remember back that far.

"You'll find out when you get older. When I'm long gone, then you'll look back and see how things change. You'll have this longer picture of time that's passed. And, too, then you'll have more time on your hands to think back over it," I finish.

Ralph says, "I know you're a thinker, John. I guess that's why I wanted to talk to you today about these problems I have."

"I know you know this, but I'll say it anyhow. We have but one chance to contribute to the greater good. We are given but one life. We have obligations and responsibilities to meet;

we can't shirk those. We all have struggles and setbacks. If sacrifice is called for, we must sacrifice. For me, the war was a sacrifice, a setback. It hobbled me, and it took me a while to regain my footing.

"Don't struggle against the times. Flow with it. Make the best of it. We have God-given talents. Like the Bible story tells us, each of us is given a talent or talents. That said, we have to use them—recognize them and kindle them, and ignite the creative forces within us.

"Don't get caught up in meaningless distraction. Stay focused and learn to flow around obstacles in order to achieve your dreams and aspirations.

"I tell you, it will all work out, Ralph. I hope maybe something I said will help."

Then I add, "Maybe you shouldn't look at them like problems. Think about them as challenges. Everybody has challenges and struggles. That's life. No matter what you do for a living."

I took a puff, then add, "I think life would be boring without them. Don't you?"

Ralph seems skeptical. For a while, I smoke and enjoy the day. Ralph is thinking things over. I am still thinking about Fogle's new, bright shiny truck as it makes a turn and vanishes around the corner.

A thought struck me, and I say to my son-in-law, "Did you know that ice used to be harvested from the Great Lakes and New England and shipped down the Hudson River? It went by steam ship everywhere. Sent down to Florida and Louisiana.

"Someone invented a cold storage area on the ship to reduce the melting, and later someone else invented a refrigerated car for the railroad. All that progress helped in the frozen water trade.

"Old man Fogle, he started with a cold storage warehouse, meat packing, then had the vision to build an ice making plant.

"It was about 1850, I can't recall the exact date. I'm forgetting a lot lately. A doctor in Florida named Gerrie invented ice making, before that ice went by boat from the Lakes. It wasn't until 1867 that we had the first commercial ice plants."

"How do you know these things, John?" Ralph looks at me, puzzled.

"I read a lot. And study.

"Aha, now I remember. It was in 1878 the glass milk bottle was patented. Changed the whole dairy business. It was invented by a druggist in Potsdam, NY. Changed everything. Ralph, a lot of exciting things have happened in my lifetime. Just because someone had an idea and took the time to work it out.

"You mark my word. The day will come when we won't need ice delivery," I finish.

"How do you know that, John?" he asks.

"I've seen some pictures of what I guess you would call an electric ice box. No ice. But keeps your food cold. They have it now, but it's not small enough for your kitchen. It's as big as a room. Probably it can be made smaller. Maybe I won't live to see it, but you will."

"Are you sure, John. You got me thinking."

"You know I like to read, Ralph, and I was sitting in there reading the other evening. When for some reason I started thinking about how in generations passed, a scribe sat in some remote monastery copying books. And the Italians, they did a vast amount of book work, copying and illuminating books. Beautiful. Works of art. That was before and during the Renaissance. It was very big business for the Italians. Can you imagine the look on a scribe's face and what a scribe must have thought when he learned that Johannes Gutenberg invented a printing press?

"I don't know why that came to my mind, but obviously the need for a scribe changed with that invention, and eventually his job became obsolete. Recently, I've been thinking about all the changes I've seen. Just think about my Ford. It's such an improvement to my life. And for everyone else who's got one.

"Henry Ford, now there's another genius. He changed the world."

"Next thing you know, someone will event a flying machine," Ralph says and laughs.

"Ralph, that's not too far-fetched. The other day I was in the shop with my car, and Harvey and his other mechanic were talking about these two young brothers out in Dayton, Ohio. They have a bicycle shop, but they are working on the concept of flying. They made a wind tunnel, even."

Ralph looks at me, incredulous. "You don't say?"

"Just ponder that for a minute. Maybe someday you could go up on some kind of flying contraption."

Ralph didn't comment, but he was thinking about it.

"I'm sure they'll have many, many problems to solve in making something fly; but if they stay with it and persist, I bet they can do it."

"Do you really think they could make a flying machine?"

"Yep, I do. People can do anything if they just put their mind to it."

"Hmmm. That's hard to fathom. Guess those fellows could change the world, too."

"Only time will tell."

"I guess so."

We both admired my Ford.

"There's a lot more to come in your generation. I won't be around to see it, but you will. You've got creative and industrious people busy changing the world forever. Like Thomas A.

Edison, there's another genius. Because of him, a housewife doesn't have to fill lamps with oil every day and clean those smoky glass chimneys. That's a time-consuming, messy job. Electricity in the house is changing everything."

Ralph nods yes in approval.

"I look at Sara's treadle sewing machine in here gathering dust, and I think, if I worked at it, I could convert that to electric. By the way, would Em like to have that sewing machine? It's one thing I need to find a home for; I won't have space for it."

Ralph says he'll ask her.

"Did you hear about Elias Howe's lawsuit for patent infringement against Issac Singer? Singer's got a mighty big business, but Howe is threatening it with legal matters," I say.

Ralph chimes in, "I'm thinking, John, if we have a nice weekend, why don't you come over to the house on Saturday, and we'll make ice cream? I'll pick up some rock salt today. The kids love ice cream, and it will keep them occupied and out of Em's hair.

"What do you say? We'll have a picnic out in the backyard. I'll throw a sheet over the clothesline and tack it down and make a tent for the kids. Em won't like it because it may put a hole in her sheet, but the kids will love it."

"They're just the right age for a clothesline tent." I smile at the thought of it.

"And, John, you can tell the kids about you being in the Union Army and sleeping in a tent. They love to hear about that."

"They do?"

"Oh, yeah. They make me tell them—what you said."

"I'll think of a story about their momma, some kind of stunt she pulled when she was their age."

"Naw, you tell them about when you were in the war. They love that."

"I really try to forget that, Ralph. I'll can tell you I was *durn* lucky if I even had a tent. Mostly, I was sleeping under the stars, or under whatever weather was coming down on us—on the cold, cold ground. Burr."

I shiver involuntarily. "I don't like to revisit that chapter in my life. It grew me up fast."

"Whatcha havin' for supper, John?" Ralph asks, as he stands up and puts his hat on.

I agree to the picnic on Sunday, and then add, "The neighbor lady brought over a pone of scrapple yesterday; she got it from a farmer down in the country. I think I'll fry some of that up."

"That sounds good," Ralph says, as he steps off the porch.

After Ralph leaves, I go into the front room and sit in my overstuffed chair. I think about all the changes that have and are taking place in my lifetime. Some inventors have come and gone on. Almost too many to enumerate: John Froehlich and his gas-powered tractor; Nickola Tesla; the Frenchman Rudolf Diesel's steam piston engine; Marconi from Bologna, Italy and his long-distance radio; the Scott, Alexander Graham Bell; Samuel Morris; and the contribution of Luther Burbank.

For me, the man of the hour is Henry Ford. "Good idea," I say right out loud. *He's changed everything. Can't say I'll ever again miss riding in a horse drawn wagon.*

I pick up Whittier's book of poetry to start all over again.

The Watchers

Beside a stricken field I stood;
On the worn turf, on grass and wood,
Hung heavily the dew of blood.
But all the air was quick with pain
And gusty sighs and tearful rain.

Two angels, each with drooping head
And folded wings and noiseless treads,
Watched by the valley of the dead.

I lay aside Whittier. My thoughts have changed from those earlier in the day, before talking to my son-in-law. My thoughts have turned to those mighty and inquiring men who left their mark on the world. Some still hard at work with their ever-evolving projects. Some deceased.

I pick up my book of Longfellow's work and leaf through the pages to the poem "Flower-de-Luce Hawthorne." This he wrote to Hawthorne's widow in 1864. Longfellow was obviously moved by the death of this creative genius. From the words of his verses, we know that Hawthorne was someone he admired and held in high esteem. What was it he said there about unfinished work?

I read the last two verses.

There in seclusion and remote from men
The wizard hand lies cold,
Which at its topmost speed let fall the pen,
And left the tale half told.
Ah! Who shall lift that wand of magic power,
And the lost clew regain?
The unfinished window in Aladdin's tower
Unfinished must remain!

Somehow, his words seem apropos.

Part Two.
At the Crossroads

The Crossroads

Ihear her coming from a long way up the lane; the dear little thing is singing to the high heavens, "Jesus loves me this I know." The precious little thing is probably wearing a matching apron and bonnet. Her mother keeps the girls nice. The family runs a productive farm. They are frugal, and so the fabric of the bonnet and apron probably comes from a remnant of her mother's dress.

Her well-worn shoes, buttoned up to the ankle, are clean and polished. The same shoes worn by her older sister a few years ago, then put up on a shelf until Molly grew into them. Of those two girls, Molly has the pleasant demeanor. A middle child she is. All are polite and well mannered; their father and mother would suffer no less.

Little blonde, curly-haired Molly visits me nearly every day, often delivering something her mother cooked or baked. In season, she carries back home the berries we pick in the woods nearby.

She's good company. At first, her mother walked her across the road to my house, and I'd walk her back. Later, I'd see her to the road and watch as she crossed, then wait until she waved to me from their kitchen door. Now she is old enough to cross the road herself.

She is inquisitive, and there is no end to questions about what I build and how it works; what makes the wheels turn or why something bobs up and down. Why does that clock tick? Why does that clock chime? At my advanced age, I have the time and leisure to marvel at her interest. I fan her curiosity.

Thinking back to the years when my own children were her age, yes, they asked questions, but I can't remember any of my girls or sons being like this child. Lately, I ask myself if I took enough time with my own. I question myself, was I too busy and self-involved in those years?

I justify to myself that in those years, I kept too busy making a living, providing for us all; truth is that with age comes patience. Now I have time to listen to Molly and answer her questions. She is a delight.

I have my own grandchildren, but they live in towns quite a distance away.

In a household with four children, her mother has a lot of work. Having had a baby this year and another under two years of age, I know she appreciates having one out of her hair for an hour or so. Then, too, Molly's aging and infirm grandmother moved in to live out her years with them. Hilda already has her hands full. She's hard-working and sometimes seems overwhelmed.

I can see the two standing on my back porch, at first. Molly holding her mother's hand and leaning against her, shyly. I'd give her a wink, and she'd blink her eyes back at me.

She's outgrown her shyness, but a couple of years later, she's still working on the winking skill.

Many times, her mother says, "John, is she in your way?" Or, "John, does she bother you?"

"No," I reply. "She is good company."

Truth is, there is nothing so pressing in my life, as it is right now, that it can't wait until the next day.

"Well, if she does, you send her right on home," Hilda says. I give Hilda a wink.

"We always find something to do here. Don't we, Molly?"

Molly nods her head, yes. Then, looking up to her mother for approval, she says, "Mister Tinker makes toys. And I help him."

"It's true. She does," I say.

"And Mister Tinker has the Peter Rabbit book, Momma," Molly sometimes adds.

"Oh, he does, does he? Well, if she's in your way, John, or if she doesn't mind her manners, you send her on home."

Hilda and I converse while Molly stands looking up at her mother, all the while tugging at her mother's skirt. Persistent with Molly's tugging, Hilda finally looks down at her with a questioning, *What is it?* look.

Something passes between them, and Hilda says, "John, Molly would like to know if you could play the Victrola phonograph today. If it's no trouble, that is."

"I think that would be a fine idea," I say.

Molly smiles and lets go of her mother's skirt.

Our properties are in rural Pennsylvania farming country, well out of town, at a major crossroads. Earlier in time, this was Indian country, and trails passed through these parts. Later, the crossroads became a stagecoach stop with overnight lodging. All that's long gone. There is scant traffic of any kind this far from town. There are quite a few hay wagons and a few buggies that pass through on any given day, but mostly it's quiet, with only squirrels and rabbits crossing the road. Only I have a motorcar.

Thomas and Hilda have always enforced a "no crossing the road" rule for their children, but in truth, there's not much danger.

Things Have Memory

I am dozing in my easy chair. Events and family matters, long passed, randomly flow in and out of my consciousness. I awaken when I hear Molly calling to me from the back porch. I get up from my chair and swing open the weathered, ill-fitting screen door.

"I brought you something," says the little girl in the bonnet.

"You did?"

"Yes, but you have to guess what it is." She stands with both hands behind her back, twisting back and forth, smiling up at me. The dimple on her right cheek is just like her mother's. With the wide smile, today, it seems deeper than usual.

"It's a surprise. You guess," she insists.

"I am surprised, and I just can't imagine what it is."

"Go on, you guess," she coaxes.

I take my time pondering. "Is it a special rock?"

She shakes her head, "No."

"A special leaf?"

"Close." She sounds like her older sister.

"Close. Hmmm. Well then, I'm a'guessing you have a flower."

"No, silly. You know that flowers are over for the year."

"Well, I guess I'll have to sit down and cogitate on it."

She gives me a questioning, uncertain look. "Mister Tinker, were you asleep?"

"No, I was just resting my eyes."

"That's what you always say. You need to guess! Put your thinking cap on, Mister Tinker." She twists back and forth some more.

"I think I'll have to give up."

She swings one arm out and shouts, "Catnip."

"Oh my. Catnip!"

She holds out a long stem of catnip, including dangling roots and earth, which has been unceremoniously ripped out of her mother's garden as she passed through on her way over here.

"Shall we have a cup of tea then?"

"Yes, please."

She comes in. The screen door slams behind us. We go to the kitchen.

"Could I have mine in the cup with the violets on it?" She adds, "Please," as if remembering that her mother would ask me if she had used her manners.

"Did she say please and thank you?" Hilda would ask.

And I could say, unequivocally, "Yes."

With the "please," she gives me a knowing look, as if we share a secret. She put both of her little hands over her mouth and snickers into them at the thought of her mother asking the same question over and over again.

I hold the strand of catnip out over the sink. "Root and all? You got it, root and all." I break the bottom third of the plant off and put it into the compost bin.

"Would you like to pick the leaves off and rinse them?" I ask.

She nods yes.

I lay a clean kitchen towel on the drain board. "Put the washed leaves on here." I pat the towel. "You do that while I heat some water to boiling."

I prime the pump, and when the water comes out and flows, I fill the kettle. The coals in the stove are still hot from breakfast. I use a poker to stir the embers. I think to myself, *I never was quite so patient with my own children. I should have indulged them more.*

But then, I did the same with my children as my father did with me. Obedience and perfection were the standard for his children. Hard work and discipline. My father was short on patience. Make something of yourself, was his usual comment.

I reach for the porcelain cup with the violets. This cup was my mothers', and it is one of those things I treasure. It was handed down from her side of the family. When I hold it, thoughts of my mother engulf me. She's been gone now for many years.

It is a fragile object, and I handle it carefully.

The catnip brews in the teapot. I put a scant teaspoonful of sugar in the cup for Molly and pour the tea. I carry her cup and a mug full for me to the parlor, which doubles as my work room.

"We have a lot of catnip leaves left. Should we dry them? Just in case we'd like some this winter. We could preserve some. What do you think of that?" I ask.

She nods her head, yes. "I think it's a good idea. We will want some this winter, and I *prob'ly* won't be able to find it under the snow."

We sat drinking our tea. I didn't say anything. I knew she had something she wanted to say.

"You're not using your mustache cup."

"No, not today."

"Momma says *things have memory*," she volunteers.

"They do," I mumble. It's almost as if she read my mind. "Your momma is a wise woman. Most people don't know that," I continue.

"Does this cup with the violets *have memory*?"

"Oh, yes."

"Does the mustache cup *have memory*?"

"Yes."

"Momma told me and Gretchen that we must keep her special silver spoon forever, and we mustn't ever lose it. It *has memory*. She only uses it at Christmas."

"Does she, now?"

"Yes. And on Easter and Thanksgiving, too."

As Molly speaks, she plays with a small bisque doll whose facial features are nearly loved off. She pulls a knit cap, a crocheted dress, and other tiny items out of her apron pocket. She tries on this and that item, in this and that way, all the while carrying on a conversation with both the doll and me.

"Do you really think *things have memory*, Mister Tinker?"

She is back to the real issue that is on her mind today.

"For certain. Go over there and look in the china cabinet. Look on the middle shelf."

She carefully pushes her cup and saucer back on the table and lays her doll things next to it. She gets to her feet and goes to the cabinet. She peers through the glass doors into the old oak cabinet. I turn to my workbench.

"You mean here where you have your front door key?"

"Yes. You see that hand-painted porcelain bird back in the corner?"

"Yes. A pincushion, isn't it?" she asks.

"Yes, it tis."

"It's a wise old owl. Isn't it? It's very lovely, even if the velvet cushion on top is mostly worn off."

"Now there then, that's a thing *that has memory*!"

"Where did you get it?" Molly asks, thoughtfully.

"It was my mother's. I think my father gave it to her. Or maybe it was that her mother got it from her mother. Maybe it came from the *old country*."

I turn back around from my work bench and look at her.

She sucks in her breath and clamps her hand over her mouth, as though she has had a great surprise and made a grand discovery.

She says, "It's a strange shape for a pincushion. I mean the spoon that *has memory*. There are flowers on the handle part. It's not like what we use every day. Mister Tinker, Momma said it was her grandmother's, and her mother brought it with her from the *old country*."

She goes back to playing with the little doll, and I turn back to the pocket watch on my workbench. She stays quietly occupied for a few minutes.

Soon she asks, "Mister Tinker, are you making an angel to add to the *'menagerie'*?" She draws the word out slowly but pronounces it properly.

"No, not right now. I'm repairing a pocket watch and a clock for a fella down the road." I turn back around and look at her over the top of my glasses with the attached watch maker's monocle. "My *menagerie*, you say?"

"That's what *you* called it," she says.

"So I did. No, I'm not working on my *menagerie* today. I'm having to make some watch parts." I turn back to the job at hand.

"Mister Tinker, do you know where the *old country* is?"

"Why yes, I do. My father came from the *old country*."

"Did you ever go there?"

"No, Molly, the *old country* is far, far away."

"But you went far, far away when you were in the war. You told me so."

"Yes, that part tis true. When I was in the war, I went as far away as Petersburg, Virginia, and Washington. I went to Chicago not too many years back, also. But the *old country* is much, much farther away than that. You have to cross the Atlantic Ocean."

Her eyes widen. "Really?" she draws out the word, pauses, almost gasps, and then continues. "Well, even so I think I'd like to go to the *old country,* some day."

"Well, then if you want to, and you think about it, and dream about it, I would say, I think you will get there. Always remember that whatever you dream of, you can achieve. When you get to be a bigger girl, that is."

"I think that would be a wonderful thing to do," she says thoughtfully.

"I do, too, but I must tell you, it would be an *arduous* journey," I tell her. I can almost see the wheels turning in her little head. I sometimes use a big word, like *menagerie*, or, today, *arduous*, deliberately.

I go on about my work as she plays and thinks about it for a while. I know her well enough to know that she is thinking *Momma says, stay out of his way, and don't be a nuisance to Mister Tinker. He won't invite you over.* I am thinking that I know, too, that she will decide to take the risk, when she asks, "Mister Tinker, what is *arduous*?"

"You don't know?" I ask.

She shakes her curly hair, "No."

"Well, first of all, you are going to have to travel all the way to a port where they have big steamships. That's already far, far away from here. Just getting to there, that's going to be *arduous*. Then, you have to go up the gangplank very carefully and get on a big ship with your trunk. Since you have to take a fair amount of clothes for the voyage, you'll be needing a trunk. Then, it's going to take a week or more on that steamship to get you to the *old country*."

"Really?" Her eyes get still wider, and she wrinkles her nose.

"Yep. *Arduous* means hard, difficult, very difficult. I heard tell that sometimes the sea is so rough that people get seasick."

"I hope that doesn't happen to me."

"I do, too, for your sake. Now, Molly, you didn't mention where you were going and how you were going to get around in the *old country*."

"Do I have to know?" She pouts.

"Well now, if you know someone who has a car like mine, someone who could pick you right up when you step off the ship and take you around, that would be somethin'."

I can see her turning the word *arduous* and other things over in her mind, engrossed in the thought of it all. Molly twists a bisque arm of her doll all the way around, then starts twisting the legs.

"Do you think they have cars in the *old country*?"

"I'm pretty sure they do."

She looks away from the doll and ventures, "Maybe they only have wagons. Or buggies."

"Hmmm, I can see you're smiling at the thought of it all. You know it will be *arduous*, but you know you will have a great time. You better start thinking where in the *old country* you are going. You're going to have to know that beforehand. So you get on the right ship."

Molly turns back to the doll and turns the dolls' arm all the way around again. She looks at me inquisitively.

I go on. "I think you should decide if you want to go to Germany, or Holland, or Switzerland. Probably, they would be my first choices, but you might want to go to Scotland, or Wales, or Ireland. What do ya think?"

"Mister Tinker, why don't you go?" she says in a near whisper, in a confidential, conspiratorial way.

"When I was young man, I thought about it. You know, Molly, even today I wish I had. I should have. I do wish I would have."

Her lip drops in a pout. "You could go, Mister Tinker. I know you could."

"I'm feeling a little too old for an *arduous* trip like that, now."

"I know you could go because you went far, far away to Chicago and to Petersburg before."

"Well now, as I told you, going there is not nearly as far away."

"How old were you when you went into the War between the States, Mister Tinker?"

"Seventeen. I just turned seventeen. I tell you, Molly, that was a long time ago. It was long before your momma and daddy were even born."

"You could have gone to *the old country* after you came back from the war."

"Well, Molly, I didn't think about it at the time. I can only tell you things were different when I came back from the war."

"You mean because of you hurt your knee?"

"Who told you that?"

"Daddy. He said you hurt your knee, and that's why you walk a little funny sometimes."

"He said that, did he? Well no, I was helping a fellow work on his barn, and I had a fall from a ladder a few years back. I didn't hurt my knee in the war, but I was hurt. Molly, are you saying that I'm gimpy?"

"Yes. A little. And you have a cane."

"Well, there is that I suppose."

"A lot of old people around here walk with a cane," she adds.

"Oh, you noticed that did you?"

"Yes, I notice them in church."

After a few moments, she says, "Daddy says you have all the *new-fangled* things."

"He said that?" I exclaim, then pause. "I wonder what he means by that?"

"You have a car. And you have Victrola. Daddy calls it a talking machine. He told me about all your 'ventions. All them are *new-fangled* things."

"Well then, I suppose I do."

I turn back to my bench work and pick up a toy angel I work on from time to time. I take the small, metal figure between my thumb and forefinger at the base and twist it ever so slightly. The halo pops up, and the wings fly out and flap up and down to Molly's delight.

"How did you do that, Mister Tinker? Let me try? Tell me how you make her fly?"

"Not now, Molly. I can't be telling all my secrets."

"You could tell me, Mister Tinker," she says quite convincingly, but with emphasize on *could*. "If you told me not to tell anyone, I wouldn't. I promise."

"Once told, a secret is not a secret. Mind you that."

"I know that. I have secrets with my sister, and I have secrets with my friends. Other secrets," she clarifies.

"Really?"

"Yep, I have a lot of secrets."

"Well, Molly, truthfully, with this angel there is a little bit of magic in it, and I wouldn't want to ruin that."

Quickly she responds as politely as she can. "Mister Tinker, are you are trying to fool me? I know there's no magic in it because you are always working hard on all these soldiers and things. And you know, magic is like this."

She snaps her thumb and middle finger together, an action she's practiced all summer. She gets a pretty good snap this time and is proud of herself.

"*Poopf.* That's magic. Magic just happens. There is no work to it at all."

"Really, is that what you think?"

Just short of being sassy, she replies, "Yes, really."

She snaps again, but this time the snap is not quite as good as the first one.

"Careful now. You see what happened to your snapper. You told your secret, and it doesn't work as well anymore." She tries again, and the next snap is worse.

"Maybe." She doesn't want to consider that.

She sighs and gathers together the doll and its clothes. "I better go home now. Momma said don't stay too long. She is making a cherry pie today. She had the cherries in the sink."

I get up from the bench and move to my comfy overstuffed easy chair, saying, "Well then, if you're going over home to help your momma with that cherry pie, I'll take a little nap and think about how I can make that angel twirl around on her own."

"Mister Tinker, you can't take a nap and think, too."

"I can. I do it all the time."

"Really? Will you tell me how?"

"I would be glad to. Maybe tomorrow," I say, as I pull my slippers off and prop my feet on the footstool. I notice my left ankle is swollen.

Molly is a very observant child who rarely misses anything. She says, "Your ankle is all *swol up* again."

"So, it *tis*."

Speaking in her mother's concerned tone of voice, she asks, "Would you like me to fetch your *lim-i-net* before I go?"

"That would be very nice of you, but no thank you, not today. It'll be okay. I don't want that horse liniment smelling up the house right now. It could interfere with my nap."

"You know, Mister Tinker, you have two soldiers been lying on your workbench who can't move, and you've been taking a lot of naps since you made them. You said they were going to doff their caps, but the caps aren't even 'tached yet."

"I know. I'm working on a plan for them, too."

"When you're sleeping?"

I lay my head back and close my eyes. "Yes," I say.

"Mister Tinker, are you kidding me?"

"Would I do that?" I raise an eyebrow. "Do you remember when I told you earlier that if you can dream it, you can achieve it?"

"Yes."

"Well, it's something like that."

"I'm gonna tell my daddy what you said."

"You do that missy, and when you come back, tell me what he says."

She reaches down and snatches the bisque doll lying askew on the floor. She put her hand on a hip and just looks at me with her big blue eyes. Then, with her most grown up airs and speaking very much in her mother's tone and manner, she opens the screen door and says, "You can be *spectin'* me 'round about six with that piece of cherry pie."

"I'll be here, just a waiting for it."

"Bye."

"Be careful crossing the road."

By the time she gets off the porch steps and to the lane, she is singing to high heavens. She goes from one tune to another, starting with "Shall we gather at the river." Then, for some reason, she changes to "This is my Father's world," then, "Leaning, Leaning, Leaning on the Everlasting Arms." She knows the verse of many songs she's learnt in church.

There is a pause in her singing before I hear a loud version of "Old Tucker." "Old Dan Tucker a-comin' to town, riding a billy-goat leadin' a hound."

Her words are garbled at this distance, but she continues with a rousing, "Get outa' my way Old Dan Tucker." Then she launches a new verse. "Old Dan Tucker was a mighty man.

Washed his face in a frying pan. Combed his head with a wagon wheel. Died with a toothache in his heal."

My oh my, I'm wondering where she got that from.

As her voice recedes up the lane, I slip into my reverie.

Molly and Mister Tinker

Molly peers through the screen door into his darkened front room and listens. She hesitates. It seems something is wrong. The clocks are not ticking. The clocks have stopped. She calls, "Mister Tinker, are you there?" There is no reply. She calls out again.

He isn't. She knows he isn't. Everything is too still.

She put a big piece of Momma's breakfast cake on the porch and runs back down the lane and across the road. She reaches home out of breath.

"Momma, Momma, something's wrong."

Hilda turns away from the sink, wiping her hands on her apron. "What's wrong, Molly?"

"Something's wrong with Mister Tinker."

"What makes you think so?"

"He doesn't answer the door. The clocks have stopped!"

"Are you sure?"

"Yes, Momma. He's not there. I called and called for him, and he didn't answer."

"Maybe he went for a walk in the cool of the morning."

"No, Momma, his boots are there."

"Are you sure?"

"Yes, Momma. The clocks are not ticking!"

With a look of concern, Hilda unties her apron strings, pulls the apron off over her head, and tosses it over a ladder-back kitchen chair. She takes the baby out of the high chair and lays him in his cradle. She tells Gretchen to watch baby Charles and to keep an eye on Anne. Her tone changes. "Now mind. You all stay in the house until I get back. Do not go outside."

As she and Molly step out of the house, she says, as much to herself as to Molly, "It's going to be a hot day, today. I already feel it."

She brushes back wisps of greying hair that escaped from the bun pinned at the back of her neck. Collecting up strays, she repositions a hairpin as they cross the lawn and head toward Tinker's house.

"When we get back, I want you to go directly to the hen house and gather the eggs. That should have been done already," she tells Molly.

"Yes, Momma," Molly says. She takes her mother's hand as they hurry across the road. The overgrown brambles along either side of Mister Tinker's lane reach out and grab her skirt.

She calls out to him with her melodic voice as they step up on his porch. She knocks on the screen door and calls out louder, but there is no reply.

"John? John? Are you in?"

Hearing no response, she tells Molly to sit on the porch swing while she goes inside.

John is slumped in his chair. The book of *Evangeline* by Henry Wadsworth Longfellow lies open on his lap to a passage which reads, "Like a phantom she came, and passed away unremembered."

Hilda comes back out almost immediately, her tone and disposition changed. She extends her hand to Molly and says quietly, "He's gone."

"Gone where, Momma?" Molly asks.

"I mean, Mr. Tinker passed away." Tears well up in her eyes. Molly doesn't understand her mother's meaning.

"Molly, please bring that plate. We'll take it with us." Molly slides off the swing, carefully picks up Mister Tinker's breakfast plate, and hands it to her mother.

Hilda puts her free arm around Molly and for a moment hugs her to her; they stand there together. Then they step off the porch. Hilda, thinking out loud, says, "We need to get back to the house. I'll need to get a message to Tinker's niece so she can contact his daughters; and somehow, I'll have to find the doctor. Molly, I know it's pretty far to walk, but do you think you could carry a note over to Mrs. Zimmerman? She will know what to do. Daddy took the wagon, and he won't be back for hours."

Molly begins to cry, although she doesn't know exactly why. Maybe it's because of the tears in her mother's eyes. She has no perception of death. "I know where Miss Tilly lives, Momma. I can go get her. I'm big enough."

At that moment, Molly feels big enough and brave enough to go down the road alone and cross several fields alone, even though she never has been allowed to before.

Tears are now streaming down her mother's face; she wipes them away with the hem of her skirt.

"Momma, Mister Tinker is telling me a story about when he was in the War Between the States. It's about how he hurt his heart when he went marching down to Petersburg, Virginia. He said they ate hardtack, and he went *fur* more 'en a week without no bacon and no eggs.

95

"Momma, did I tell you we are working on two new soldiers for the water wheel?" Molly keeps talking. Her mother nods but isn't answering her.

As they near the back porch, they hear the baby fussing. His first tooth is coming in. Although, not comprehending the situation with her friend, Mr. Tinker, and somewhat confused, Molly is feeling quite grown up for the moment and thinks, *We had that with baby Anne, too.*

Momma said Mister Tinker passed away, but what does that mean? Molly knows that something is different, and something is wrong.

"Now we won't finish, and now I won't hear the end of the story." Molly falls into her mother's arms, sobbing and slobbering. Hilda rubs her back, stroking her hair to soothe her.

Molly can't stop crying, saying over and over again, "Mister Tinker is my friend. He is the nicest person alive. We didn't finish the story. He has to finish the soldiers."

Molly stomps her feet and bawls about all their unfinished business until her mother finally says firmly, "Straighten up now, Molly. Let me wipe your face. Hurry now and take this note to Mrs. Zimmerman."

The obituary lists the names of his parents, brothers, and sister, his wife deceased, and his children. It mentions his life work, contributions to the community and the church, of which he was a member; but to all the children of this rural Pennsylvania community, and to all the locals who didn't know him when he was a young man, he was known as Tinker or Mr. Tinker.

His proper name was John David Weaver. He raised a large family and was a successful businessman, with a fine reputation, who contributed to society. At some point over the ensuing years, the name "Tinker" was pinned on him, and it stuck.

Maybe it was because of his work on the hydraulic ram or his fascination with the automobile.

In truth, he did a fair amount of tinkering. A modest man, most people were not aware, he had two patents registered with the US Patents Office. Thus, over time, his proper name faded into the past, and so he came to be known as Tinker. Molly came to know and understand this only after his death.

A stream meandered right next to the cottage that Weaver bought when he chose country living and moved from town. He built a water wheel there. He explained to Molly that it could generate power before she was old enough to understand, as were most of the other little kids who visited. All they knew was that the toys in the house had something to do with the turning of the water wheel. For the younger ones, he explained it as magic. For the older and more curious boys, he took the opportunity to explain waterpower—that a cam turns a wheel, and some other fundamentals about waterpower and hydraulics. To some extent, the water wheel stood as a joyful symbol of his life's work.

When Mr. Tinker let it, the wheel went around and around. It dipped into the stream and magically turned small figures in his house. Like the other little girls, Molly was fascinated with the spilling water outside and more fascinated with the figures that moved, danced, pirouetted, and turned in the workshop. More than once little Molly's momma had to take her home because she got so engrossed with the action of the toys and playing in the cool water, she forgot herself and tinkled her underpants, as she watched—enthralled.

When Molly got a little older, she spent a lot of time at Tinker's house, only a short walk from hers. Tinker told her that whenever he had an idea, he went to carving it in wood or making the metal figures. When the water wheel in the stream went around and around outside, inside the bells tinkled and dinged, unicycle wheels turned, hands waved and figures bowed, delighting all who came to visit.

He patiently answered her questions and all those who showed curiosity.

You could say Mister Tinker fascinated Molly. Conversely, Molly fascinated him. As a five-year-old, she had no end of questions, which he patiently answered, or explained, even though she did not quite understand.

Mr. Tinker built and repaired clocks and watches for people. From early childhood, Molly liked to stand beside his workbench to see what he was doing. He didn't seem to mind kids or others looking over his shoulder.

Molly fairly beamed whenever Mr. Tinker said to her mother, "Let her stay awhile. I'll walk her back over in a little while." He'd eat the pie Molly's momma baked. Then he'd wash his plate in his sink, take Molly's hand, and walk her home. If it was muddy in the lane, he picked Molly up so her shoes wouldn't get dirty.

According to Molly, Mr. Tinker was a very nice man and her best friend. He told her that when she got a little older, he'd teach her to fix clocks. Molly played dolls with her friends, but with Mister Tinker, they did real important things. Like they walked in the woods and picked berries and collected wild edibles, and then he'd give them to Momma, and she'd fix them for supper. He knew everything about wild edibles, and in the summer, he knew the best places to find black berries, elderberries, and raspberries and where to catch fish.

The Model T

Molly is in the barn. All morning long she fiddled around in there, not doing anything of any account. She acts like this—dithering—when she has something on her mind.

Her father, Thomas, heaves the last of the hay bales up on to the wagon, straps them down, and goes into the barn to talk to her.

Molly is sitting on the passenger's side of old man Weaver's Model T, which he's kept there, stored, protected from the weather. The death of the old man is clearly troubling her. In the last couple years, the years of his decline, the two had become best buddies and confidants. Now he is gone, and Molly is experiencing the loss and not dealing well with her grief. Thomas asked Hilda to talk to Molly, to help her get through this difficult period. She did, but there hasn't been much improvement.

Thomas has a standing rule that no one is to touch the Model T, and there is an unsaid understanding to kids and all visitors to the Miller's farm that if someone were to touch it, there would be serious consequences. But there sits Molly on the front seat. It's as if this is all she has left of him.

Sometimes Weaver paid Thomas a little money for allowing him space to park the car, protected in his barn. Mostly Weaver brought things back from his trips—a bushel of apples, a sack of walnuts, soap, a peck of whatever he found. He knew gifts of this sort would be well received and used by Thomas and his family.

During these years of country living, Weaver travelled far and wide, visiting with family members, mostly his daughters, while continuing to install and repair the hydraulic rams he invented, often with his brother Henry. Thomas knew Weaver often took fruit, vegetables, and other items of barter in lieu of payment. His brother Henry didn't like that and outwardly expressed his disapproval. But that was then. Thomas smiles just remembering how Weaver had loved this car.

About two years ago, John had taken a serious fall from a ladder. He wrenched his back and had troubles with his neck. He hadn't driven as much after that.

Today, Thomas ignores his own rule and gets in on the driver's side. He rubs his hands, admiringly, over the fine upholstery and the steering wheel, then pops right out with it. "So, sis, what are you thinking?"

Molly's usual smile is gone, and her big blue eyes are watery. "I am thinking why did Mister Tinker have to die? He was my very best friend and a very nice person. There are plenty of crabby mean old men, and woman, too, who shout at kids and run them off with their rake or a hoe if they so much as cross over their property or take a shortcut through their field. Why don't they die? Mister Tinker was a nice man."

"Wait, sis, that's two things. First of all, nobody gets to pick when it's time to go. When it's time to pass. And, secondly, I think you should be more respectful of older people. You wouldn't know this, but lots of elderly folks have aches and pains. You know, rheumatism and arthritis. Their joints hurt from the weather and from use over the years. Think about that *fur* a minute. Maybe that's the reason they are 'crabby,' as you say."

"Or maybe some people were just born mean."

"Now, sis, that's not nice talk, and I won't stand for you talking like that. I know you feel bad because Mister Tinker died, and if you want to talk about it, well that's why I came in here. Just to sit with you *fur* a spell and talk. If you want to."

"Why did everybody at the funeral call Mister Tinker, 'John,' and the preacher called him Mr. John D. Weaver? Isn't his name Mister Tinker?"

"I know everybody around here calls him *Tinker*, you are not wrong about that. I suppose you could say that Tinker was a name he earned, but his proper name, his given name, was John D. Weaver. 'D' is for David."

Thomas waits for Molly to reply, but she doesn't. "Sis, you have to admit he did a lot of tinkering. You remember he was an inventor, don't you? He had that hydraulic ram he invented and was always tinkering with that, improving on it. Maybe you were too little to remember how he used to come over here and tinker with this car. After he tinkered with it for a couple days, he would pack up a few things and drive on over to visit his daughter and his grandbaby in Danville. Well, all that was before you can remember."

Molly listens to what her daddy is saying but doesn't respond. Thomas is doing his best to lift her spirits.

"Molly, did I ever tell you that once Mr. Tinker came all the way across the road just to tell me he had found another way not to do it?

"I ask him what he meant by that. He was talking about that hydraulic ram he invented. You know how he was always working on it, trying to improve upon it.

"Then he told me that it is just as important to know what doesn't work as it is to know what does work! That really got me thinking. You know, he was always working and drawing stuff out and well, tinkering. You saw that."

"Yes, he made a lot of drawings and *speriments*, he called them."

"Yes, experiments. So, Molly, that's how he earned the name 'Tinker,' and over time, people just forgot about his real name. At the funeral, everyone was being particularly respectful, and they used his proper name."

Molly looks up at her father. "Daddy, I didn't know Mister Tinker had so much family, I mean, that many daughters. Why didn't they ever come to see him?"

"Well, they did come, some. I am sure there were many reasons."

"Like what?" she asks.

"Well, like they all live in other counties."

"So?"

"Well," says Thomas. "I'm not making excuses or nothing for them, but I figure most of them have children to look after and work that keeps them at home. And his daughter, Miss Alice, you've met her—she has a really big farm with cows and pigs. You know that with a farm, you've got many chores. That keeps ya busy night and day, and you can't just leave and go off for a day. Who would slop them pigs? Who would gather them eggs and feed them chickens? Maybe they don't have a buggy to haul themselves over here. I know Miss Amelia and Will have a motor car, but I doubt they all do. Anyhow, you know Mr. Weaver often went to visit them. Did you know he had the first Model T in this county?"

Thomas continues to rub the steering wheel lovingly and admires the vehicle. "This must have cost him a pretty penny."

"What's going to happen to it?" Molly asks.

"I spoke to his son-in-law, who knows how to drive. He works in a machine shop, and he's learning how to fix cars. He said he'd get a ride over here in a week or so and pick it up."

Molly starts to cry. "You mean they are going to take his car away?"

"Yes." Thomas lets that settle in.

Molly whimpers and says, "Some ladies took things from his house after the funeral. In fact, they've taken away just about everything. I was over there with Momma, and we saw them."

"Well, those ladies were his daughters and his nieces, and that's the normal thing to do when a person passes."

"What will happen to the water wheel? They took his books and most of the clocks and the soldiers. And his daughter, Missus Amelia from Danville, took the model of his ram that he keeps in a black case up on the mantel. They only left the pocket watches and soldiers we were working on—the ones in pieces. The ones that didn't work, yet."

"I'm sure he would want you to have them. I'll ask his son if it would be all right for you to have them."

"Daddy, they didn't take the portrait over the fireplace."

"Well, maybe it was too big to cart home, or maybe some-one will come *fur* it later. Maybe they don't have room *fur* it in their house."

"Daddy, if they don't take it, do you think we could keep it?"

"Well, Molly, with that big oak frame and all—it's really big."

She gives her daddy a pouty face.

"I'll have to talk to your mother about it. Where would we put it?"

"If we can't put it in the house, maybe we could put it right here in the barn." She points.

"There's space for it right up there above them bridles. What do you think, Daddy?"

"Well, I'll have to ask your mother."

"You know Momma doesn't care what we do in the barn. I'm sure she would think it's just fine. I'm going to ask her." She flounces down off the seat. Before Thomas can say, "Watch your fingers," she carefully closes the car door behind her and runs off toward the house.

Thomas goes back to work, hoping the talk has helped and that he won't hear her sniffling tonight at bedtime, as she has been. *Not sure how you can replace a guy like that—a one of a kind, a touch of genius, a creative mind, a good thinker that "tinker,"* Thomas thinks.

Her grieving persists, and two days later, when Thomas comes in from the field, he finds Molly sitting in the Model T again. This time she is on the driver's side. Since their last con-versation, Thomas has thought about this more and discussed the problem with Hilda again. Hilda felt they should just let her talk it out with both of them. They decided that whenever it comes up, they'd be open and frank about John's death and reinforce all the good things that they, as adults, know about him. As Hilda points out, Molly has no experience with death except for the one horrific week when Laddy died. But getting a new puppy the next week resolved that. The death of Tinker will not be easily resolved.

"Hi, sis, whatcha been doin' today?"

"Me and Momma walked over to Martha's for a visit. I pushed Charles in the pram. Momma baked bread, and we took 'em a loaf. Martha and I played dolls and cut out paper dolls while her momma and Ms. Gertrude and Mrs. Howell quilted. That's all."

"Hmmm. That sounds like a lot of playing. I think I should take you out in the field with me, let you do a good day's work, let you work up a good lather."

Molly is holding back her tears. She drops her chin to her chest, looks away, and says, "I wanted to go over to see Mister Tinker today and finish up those soldiers we were working on. But he's not there, you know? And his house is probably locked up."

Thomas pats on his daughter's arm reassuringly and gently flattens out the folds of her skirt, which hang down over the seat. Molly is a child with a sweet disposition, and he hates to see her troubled like this.

"I've been thinking about your friend, Mister Tinker. You are right. He was a really special person. Of course, you know he was a very smart man, and he did some very interesting things in his life. Things I bet he never mentioned to you because you two were always so busy with one project or another."

She looks up at her father inquiringly, as if to say, *Like what?*

"Yep. A long time ago, he told me about when he fought in the War Between the States. He was only a young man. About nineteen, I think he said. I bet he never told you that?"

105

"Yes, he did, too, tell me that, but he was seventeen. Not nineteen. One time when his knee was all puffed up, he told me it had been 'no darn good' ever since the war. He told me he hurt his knee and his heart in the war."

"That's what Tinker said?" Molly's daddy questions.

"Yes."

"Well then, I guess you know all about that then."

She adds, "He called it his 'bum leg.' Didn't you see how he limped when it hurt sometimes?"

"I guess I wasn't paying attention."

"He said his leg wasn't half as bad as his father-in-law's was. I think it was his father-in-law, or one of his relations, 'cause he told me about when he was in the war, too. He told me that fellow hurt it when they were having a *charge*. Mister Tinker wasn't there when it happened, but he heard tell that they were running through some woods out in Virginia when that fellow went over a pile of logs and his foot slipped in between them and he wrenched his knee right out of the socket.

"Mister Tinker said his relations couldn't walk at all then. So, some other soldiers or his friends or someone carried him back to the field hospital for them to look at it. The doctor said it was so bad that they wrapped it up and put him out of the army. Because they couldn't fix it back right."

"That's what Mister Tinker said?"

"One day we were tramping around out in the woods hunting for elderberry bushes, and some loggers left some stacked up logs out there in a pile, and I was going to climb up on them. I didn't because Mister Tinker said 'no,' and he said there might be snakes there, too. We found the elderberries, but they weren't ripe for picking yet. When we walked back home, he told me about his father-in-law's bum leg. Said it happened in the war.

"Daddy, how old is seventeen?" Molly asks.

"Well, you know Bobby Trutt, down the road?" Thomas responds.

"Yes. He's a pretty big boy," she replies.

"I think he just turned seventeen this year. Yep, he is a pretty big boy."

Thomas says, "I have an idea, sis, let's go the house and see what Momma made for supper. I'm half-starved, aren't you?"

Molly shakes her precious little head, no, and the curls flop around. "No, I had some ginger snaps a while ago."

"Did you save one for me?" Thomas asks.

Molly breaks into a mischievous smile.

"I can't believe you didn't save one for me!" Thomas gives her his gruff look. "Of course you're not hungry. You have no appetite because you haven't done a lick of work all day. Tomorrow, you're going to the field with me. I'm taking you like a sack of wheat."

Thomas picks Molly up and slings her over his shoulder.

Molly starts squalling and kicking. "No, Daddy; no, Daddy; no, Daddy!"

At the backdoor, Thomas puts her down. She runs into the house justa *hollerin'* her head off. "Momma, Momma, save me."

Thomas sits on the porch steps, smiling and listening to the ruckus, as he pulls off his boots and knocks off the loose dirt. Then he goes inside.

Molly is clinging to her mother, laughing and squealing with her face hidden in her mother's skirt.

Playfully, Hilda looks at Thomas sternly. "What are you doing to my child?"

"He's gonna make me work in the field," Molly says. "Save me, Momma."

Hilda pries Molly loose and goes back to the cook stove, lightly stirring cooking vegetables. Then, in a half-serious tone, she says, "It's like this, Molly, you can work in the field with your daddy, or you can work with me in the kitchen."

Hilda and Thomas exchange glances. Hilda doesn't like it when Thomas roughhouses with the girls, especially at mealtime or at bedtime. She says it gets them overexcited.

Picking up a wooden spoon, Hilda says, "Thomas, I am going to take this spoon to you if you don't let this child be."

Hilda looks at Molly, who is laughing and breathless. "And you, I'm taking your silence to mean you want to help me in the kitchen. So, Miss Molly, you go wash your hands, put your apron on, and then set the table. Supper will be ready soon."

Keeping her eyes on her daddy, Molly put her hands over her mouth to hide her laughter at getting her daddy in trouble.

Still snickering, she goes over to the child size wooden clothes tree that stands in the corner. It holds assorted bibs and aprons and bonnets, most of which have been stitched by her grandmother. She reaches up to the peg that is exactly within her grasp and snatches hers.

Meeting the Wizard

A busy day is winding down for the Miller family. Evening light casts long shadows outside as the late afternoon sun retreats.

Hilda goes from the dining room to the front room, closing the windows to trap the warmth of the day. She pulls the blinds three quarters of the way down, as is her usual evening routine. The remains from supper have not yet been cleared away, and the dishes have yet to be washed and dried. Then, for her, there are four children to get ready for bed.

"Are you feeling all right, Molly?" Molly's mother asks. As she passes her chair, she gently pats her shoulder.

Molly looks down; tears blur the mashed potatoes and green beans left on her plate.

She repeats, "Molly. Momma asked you, are you feeling all right?"

"Yes." Molly's reply is muffled. She doesn't look up.

Hilda and Thomas exchange glances. They have a way of communicating without words around the children, and the message from Hilda is, *Thomas, you deal with this.*

"Molly," her father says, "you haven't touched your supper. Is everything okay? Is something wrong?"

Hilda smooths the tablecloth with the flat of her hands several times like she does every time she is about to say something, even though there *weren't wrinkles one* to smooth out. She looks at Thomas, as if to say, *Daddy's intervention is required here,* or *I give up, it's your turn.*

"You look a little peaked," Hilda says to Molly. She puts the back of her hand against their second child's forehead. "You don't seem to have a fever. Are you all right?"

Molly looks up and says straight out, "I met a wizard."

"A what?" her astonished mother asks.

"A wizard."

"What pray tell is a wizard?" Hilda asks.

"Well." She twists the napkin on her lap and seems totally without words.

Molly knew that sooner or later, she was going to have to tell them about the wizard, but at that moment she is without an explanation—but at least she has said it. It is out. Spilling this out is actually a relief. Molly is not good at keeping secrets, and she has held this one in for a few days.

Her mother has an accusatory look. "Where? Where did you meet this wizard?

"Over by the stream," Molly ventures.

Hilda looks at Thomas.

"What stream?" she asks Molly.

"You know. By the *crick* where the Indians used to come?" Molly replies.

"You mean a long time ago before neither you nor I was born. That *crick*?" Thomas asks.

"Yes, that *crick*," Molly says, as she squirms in the chair and fiddles with her spoon.

"You don't need to be going there," her mother says firmly and to the point.

"Well, Mr. Tinker and I became blood brothers there; so, I sort of do need to be going there—sometimes," Molly says.

Although surprised at the "wizard" remark, Thomas shakes his head ever so slightly in disbelief. He senses a need to be understanding and gentle in this matter. Before falling off to sleep the other night, he and Hilda discussed that neither of them are sure what is going through Molly's head. Unlike her younger siblings, who are too young to understand that their neighbor died, or like the older Gretchen, who experienced the death of their grandparents a few years back, Molly is dealing with grief for the first time. That alone is enough to bear, but Molly and Tinker had spent a lot of time together over the last couple of years.

Molly says rather sheepishly, "Momma, I know you don't believe it, but there really was a wizard there."

"You're right. I'm not believing it." Hilda stands firm.

Gretchen snickers in amusement and goes off to the kitchen with her plate.

Hilda has apparently forgotten her conversation with Thomas on the matter, which ended with a promise that they would tread lightly with Molly and be open to any conversation if the subject of John Weaver came up. Thomas leans forward and gives Hilda a steady look, but she totally misses his unspoken message.

"Vate vonce, Hildie." Thomas's vernacular lapses into his German origins. "Let Molly say want she needs to. There is no harm in hearing her *ought*."

He turns to Molly and asks, "So now, Molly, what happened?"

"Well, I was wading," she offers.

Distracted by all that is happening at the table with the other children, Molly's mother doesn't catch Thomas' nonverbal message, and she persists.

She raises her voice in an unyielding and somewhat distraught tone, saying, "My heavens, Molly! You had your shoes off in this weather? You were wading in icy cold water this time of year?"

Hilda stands up abruptly and loudly stacks two serving bowls one on top of the other with the remains of fried potatoes and applesauce. The thought of nursing a sick child back to health irritates her. So much so that she clearly breaks the rule she taught the girls of not stacking food bowls together. She makes a move to take them to the kitchen.

"It wasn't that cold, Momma."

"You'll catch your death!" a distraught Hilda says.

"Gretchen." Thomas directs his words to his oldest daughter, who appears from the kitchen. "Please help your mother clear the table." Then he continues. "Now, what happened, Molly?"

While looking at Molly and waiting for an answer, he pulls the straight back chair next to him and away from the table a little, thus allowing enough space to let his next younger child, Anne, get down. A cushion on the chair, which allows her to sit higher at the table and also serves to cover the broken cane seating, slides out from beneath her. Thomas holds the little child firmly by her arm, averting a tumble, helping her get down, and then steadying the wobbly and frail blue-eyed child.

When she is standing solidly upright, he tussles her hair and pats her lightly on the rump. "Anne, be a big girl and run along. You help Momma and Gretchen in the kitchen." He knows that if he is to get to the bottom of this, it will be best to clear the dining room by hustling everyone off to the kitchen and evening chores.

The last of his four children sits in a highchair, bald and also blue-eyed; he babbles and blows bubbles. He has applesauce liberally around his mouth, on his face, and in his sparse, fair hair. He is happy busily pounding his spoon on the tray table.

Well, close enough. I can deal with that music, Thomas thinks. Hopefully baby Charles will not realize that Hilda left the room and commence to squalling. Thomas knows that soon enough, Hilda will be back to clean up the baby and the chair, too.

"Now, Molly, as best you can, tell me what happened," her father asks calmly.

"Papa, I was just wading. I was pushing around some leaves that were floating with a stick. I made a dam. Then I got out and sat on the big, flat rock over there. You know the rock I mean?"

Hilda returns, obviously distressed. She shuffles things around and collects some plates and serving bowls. "I can't believe you and Mr. Tinker cut your fingers and did that blood brothers thing."

Molly seems perturbed that she had to admit it. "Momma, it was only pretend."

"Hilda, please sit down or clear the table or do whatever you need to do, but let's allow Molly to tell her story."

Hilda leaves.

"Papa, it's not a story. It's the truth." She hangs her head.

He says, "Okay, so you were sitting on the flat rock. I hope you were putting your shoes and socks back on because your mother is right about that. It's not summer. You could get pneumonia and—" He almost said, "you could die," but he caught himself. The last thing he wanted to do was to resurrect more memories of Tinker dying. "—so what happened next?"

"I heard a voice," she says quietly.

"Really?" Her father draws in a deep breath.

"You heard a voice?" He exhales.

"He was speaking in real good English. He wasn't from around here; I could tell because he wasn't speaking Dutch-ified, and he had a very friendly voice."

"Molly, you know the rules about talking to strangers, but I'd rather know what he was wearing. Was he dressed for winter?"

The question seems to stump Molly. "Okay, never mind about that. Go on," he encourages her.

"Well, Papa, he was sitting on a limb overhanging the *crick*. I think he just wanted to talk to me about Mr. Tinker—I mean Mr. Weaver. You know, about Mr. Tinker dying."

Well, now she's said it. That's a good thing.

Hilda emerges from the kitchen and goes to the sideboard, picks up her grandmother's fancy candy dish that came from the *old country*, and places it in the center of the table. She situates the salt and peppershaker, a pepper grinder, and a sugar bowl next to it—*just so*. She steps back to admire the bowl, a family heirloom, and says, "What did he look like? Tell your father what he looked like."

"Just normal," Molly replies.

Her mother goes on. "Normal? Just normal? Would that be normal for a person or normal for a wizard? Because, Molly, I seriously do not know what a wizard looks like, and I'm sure your daddy doesn't either. You need to explain yourself, young lady."

"Well, he wasn't dressed for winter because he said he wasn't staying long."

"Really? So, you're saying no overcoat and no galoshes?" Walking around the table, Hilda gathers up soiled napkins for washing, piling them into a heap. She then turns her attention to the drumming baby. She uses a damp washcloth to wipe the baby's face. She kisses him on the top of his little bald head, and with some resistance, takes his spoon away. Then one by one, she carefully wipes each tiny finger clean.

The music stopped, finally, Thomas is thinking. Hilda expertly extracts the baby from the highchair and gathers up the napkins for the laundry.

"Papa," Molly continues, "wizards come, and wizards go. Wizards move around a lot."

Hilda rolls her eyes at her husband. He slightly shakes his head, signaling her not to interrupt. Molly's words trail her mother back into the kitchen.

In all seriousness, Molly says, "Papa, mostly real people never see wizards; it's only unless they want to be seen."

"Aha! That's it," Thomas says.

These are the words her father always uses to acknowledge he hears and understands what is being said. "Aha" is the word that implies that he expects to hear more because either he does not agree at all or maybe he doesn't exactly agree. Sort of like when you forget your schoolwork, or you haven't gone to the hen house—yet—and you haven't collected the eggs but you intend to do so.

Molly seems a little defeated, as if she has stepped into something never having thought about having to use her words to explain her experience, and so she restates. "Papa, unless the person wants to see the wizard and unless the wizards wants to."

"Okay, Molly, from what I hear you saying, the wizard was up in the tree."

"Yes."

"All the time?" he asks.

"No, he walked 'round sometimes, too. 'Specially when he was *splaining* things. And also—"

Her father interrupts her because he wants Molly to tell him that the wizard hadn't laid a finger on her. "Like explaining what?" he asks.

"Well mostly about Mr. Tinker. About Mr. Weaver."

"What did he say about Tinker?"

"He knew everything about him. Papa, he knew about his *'ventions*. He called Mister Tinkers *'ventions* his 'life's work,' is what he called it. He said Mister Tinker's work had helped lots of people. He said I had no idea just how many. He said Mister Tinker was a very smart man, and he used his 'intelligence and creativity' is what he called it, to make *'ventions* to improve the lives of the folks living around here and down in the country."

"Hmmm. Really?"

Then, almost in a whisper, as if to confide in her daddy, Molly says, "Papa, he even knew about Mister Tinker being in the War Between the States. He told me that even after that, Mister Tinker always had heart troubles; and, Papa, he said that is why his feet *swole* up." She nods her head in the affirmative.

"Is that so? The wizard told you that?"

All in one breath she says, "He told me that Mister Tinker built the clock that's on the mantle over at his place; and he made the outside and all the parts inside it; and it was in the World's Fair; and Mister Tinker traveled far, far way to see it."

"Yes, he did. I knew that. That clock was shown at the World's Fair," Thomas says.

"You never told me that. Mister Tinker never told me that." She seems a little bit put out with me, or disappointed in Tinker.

116

"You know, Mr. Tinker was not a boastful man, and, Molly, I can't always remember to tell you every single thing I know. Things that happened way before you were born. If I did, you'd know everything I know, and everything you know, and that would make you smarter than me." Thomas smiles at her in a secretive manner.

Then a sly little smile formed at the corners of Molly's lips.

Thomas says, "I will tell you something I bet you didn't know. In the front room on your mother's piano is a music leaf turner. Mr. Tinker built one for your momma long before you were born."

"Really?"

"Yes. Mr. Tinker invented the music leaf turner and something else you probably don't know. His inventions are registered in the Patent Office of the United States of America in Washington. Isn't that something?"

Changing the subject, she begs, "Daddy, can we go to Washington and see them? Please."

Seeing a "no" coming, Molly adds, "Someday?"

"Well, we'll see about that," Thomas says.

"Papa, did you know Mister Tinker had twelve children?"

"I didn't know exactly. I never stopped to count them up, but you know some of them. He has one daughter in Danville, that's Amelia, and another one over in Milton. You've met Miss Alice; she has a big farm down in the country, near Northumberland. He'd take this motorcar out for a drive and drive over to see them. He drove all the way to Renova, Pennsylvania to see his daughter, Bertha. They came by to see him from time to time, too. Maybe you didn't realize that Missus Ida is another of his daughters. And he has grown grandchildren, too."

"I didn't know that. I remember when Buddy came to stack wood, and Mister Tinker didn't want it stacked so close to the house 'cause of snakes. And he wasn't stacking it right neither, but he wouldn't take any tellin', and they had an argument about it," she says.

"Who won?" her father asks snidely.

"Mister Tinker won. Anyway, I thought Buddy should have been more *'spectful.*"

"Molly, you never told me what this wizard fellow was wearing. Did he have a cap? Was he wearing a sweater? Was he wearing overalls? Now then, tell me how you would describe him."

She seems to be thinking about it.

Thomas tries again. "Take your time, Molly. Was he tall, short? Was he my size?"

"Oh, Papa, no. I told you he was sitting on a branch. If he was your size, he would have broken it." At her words, she gave Thomas a big smile, covered her mouth with both hands, and laughed at the thought of it.

"Okay, then you're saying he was small?"

"Yes, maybe about my size. No, maybe as big as Gretchen. Yes, he was 'bout as big as Gretchen, but with a few more muscles. Even though he was as tall and skinny, just like Gretchen."

"You saw his muscles?"

"Yes, I guess." Molly looks dubious about what she's just said.

"Now, Molly, I am worried about this. Who was this person? What business did he have in these here parts? Did he have a name?"

"I think he did." She thinks about it for a moment but can't offer a name.

118

"Maybe he didn't tell me, Papa; it's not really that important. He just came to tell me that my blood brother was fine where he was. 'A' 'O' 'K' is what he said. That's when he was walking around. He picked my stick up and used it to draw the letters 'A' 'O' 'K' in the mud.

"I can show you the letters tomorrow, if it doesn't rain," she suggests.

She continues. "Then somehow or other, when I wasn't looking, he got back up there on the branch. He just sat there on the limb with his skinny legs and feet dangling over the *crick*.

"Papa, I don't want to be rude, but you know how Mrs. Clowser always says, 'Lawzie, hain't you a sight for sore eyes?' Well, being up there like that and all, he was a sight for sore eyes!"

Thomas hears the screen door slam. Hilda is taking the children out on the porch. It will soon be bedtime. She will rock at least one, maybe two to sleep.

"He just sat there on the limb, and I just sat there on the flat rock for a long time. It was all quiet. We were thinking, and we weren't saying nothin'. I mean, we weren't saying anything. Just thinking.

"Oh yes, I remember. He said, life is a journey, remember who you meet along the way."

"Who was he talking about?" Thomas asks.

"I'm not for sure. He said a meeting is no coincidence."

"Was he talking about himself or Mr. Tinker?"

"I don't know. Then, Papa, this is what he said. He said, 'Miss Molly, see those bubbles?' And I looked where he pointed, and, Papa, there were all these tiny bubbles floating along, like I never saw in the *crick* before.

"He said, 'Miss Molly, remember we are all just like that—bubbles in a stream.'

"Papa, I was going to ask him how he made all those bubbles happen. Because you know if it were from a fish, there would only be one bubble. Right?"

She nods her head, as if to convince herself of what she was saying. "There were so many bubbles it *kunda* been from a fish, Papa. There were lots of little baby bubbles coming up and bigger bubbles popping. And more and more were coming up all the time, and they were pretty; some just floated right on past me down the stream."

Her father wasn't sure what to make of the fairy tale Molly was telling him, and he wasn't sure how to handle it, either. He didn't speak. He just studied her, and she went on.

"Daddy, when I looked back up, he was gone. He just vanished into the branches. I called and called. But, Daddy, I think he is gone. Gone for good. Really, Daddy."

With tears welling up in her eyes, her father says, "Come here and sit on my lap."

Molly moves off her chair. She is crying now. This one hasn't been on Thomas' lap for what seems to be a long time. He pulls her over and settles her on his lap. It seems she has grown quite a bit when he wasn't looking. Crowded out by the smaller ones, she is getting to be a lap full. Thomas wipes her tears. He puts his arms around her and hugs her, tenderly rubbing her thin little arm and shoulder.

Molly sobs out the words, "Daddy, he's not coming back, is he?"

"If he does, Molly, I want you to come tell me right away," Thomas says.

"No, Daddy, I mean Mister Tinker. He's not coming back, is he?"

"Right, sweetheart. He's not coming back."

Molly and the Way West

Molly knows her momma and daddy don't believe a word she's said about the wizard. She sees how they look at her, and she sees how they looked at each other at supper. So, she didn't tell them everything the wizard told her. She didn't tell Gretchen either because Gretchen probably would have laughed at her and told Momma.

Molly snuggles deeper under the covers. Momma came in earlier and put the down-filled comforter on the bed because she was shivering. The bed is getting warmer, but her feet are still cold. The house is still except for the clock in the hall downstairs, which is chiming nine o'clock, but Molly lost count around the sixth chime. She knows her big sister, sleeping next to her, is sound asleep. She can tell by her breathing noise. That's how she knows.

She is wishing she could talk to Mister Tinker about the wizard because he would understand, but he died. So, she can't.

Before falling asleep, Molly needs to remember what the wizard said about how to get to the Lake of the Crescent Moon. This is very important. She needs to remember it for a long time—until she grows up. She can't ever forget. *It's going to be a while until then*, she is thinking—that is, until she will be big enough to go—because it is far, far away.

She rubs her feet together. They are still cold but getting warmer.

The wizard told her how to get there. He said he came from there; and to get back there, you just do what he did—only in reverse. That makes sense. He said travel west across the vast continent of North America to reach the great waters of the Pacific Ocean. He said, there, you hire yourself out to a ship captain or pay your way to Peking. He said in future days, they will call Peking, Beijing, but don't be confused. When you arrive there, in Peking, you are in China. Head south. For a few coins, you can join a Chinaman and his family on his small boat. Mind you, he said, the whole family lives on a small boat. But he said he thought they would have room enough for her. He said mix with the scholars and the regular folks. He said eat the vegetables they cook. Be sure to see the silk worms in Suzhou, and see the commerce along the way.

"Alas, the Grand Canal has fallen somewhat into disrepair," the wizard told her. "Arrive in Shanghai and have a look around. Hopefully, you will meet up with some travelers headed west. See the jugglers and the acrobats there; they are remarkable," he said.

"This will be a good place to join up with some other folks and travel overland to Xian."

He told her to remember that the Chinese name *Xian* is pronounced like She-On, and she should try to remember that. "Xi sounds just like your word 'she,'" he said.

He told her that when she got to She-On, "It's easy to join a caravan and head west." He said, "The journey is *arduous*." And she knew what *arduous* meant because Mister Tinker told her that getting to *the old country* was *arduous*.

It was hard to remember all this and to keep it all straight. But the wizard said with any luck she would reach Lanzhou, which is on the edge of the Gobi Desert. He said from there, it's not far at all to reach the oasis of Dunhuang and the Mingsha Mountain. There, she would find the Lake of the Crescent Moon.

"Mind you," the wizard said, "you have to ride on a camel." He said that since there weren't any camels around here, there was no way to practice; for her, camel riding probably would be the *arduous* part. He also cautioned that if she met up with any ruffians along the way, not to talk to them.

The wizard went on and on about the "singing sands" of the Gobi. Molly puzzled over that. She couldn't imagine how sand could sing. He told Molly that the people there were gaily dressed. Not in plain clothes and bonnets, like around here in Pennsylvania. He said their hats and vests might be embellished with tiny bells that jingle as they walk. Imagine that.

The wizard reminded her that these directions were the reverse of how he got here. Then he added that there was another way to get there, and he had gone that way, too. That would be the "across the pond" way.

He told Molly, "If you prefer, you could strike out across the Atlantic Ocean. Then, from *the old country*, you find your way to Tyre, and then through Central Asia." He said there was a vast desert called the Taklimakan. He said the food there was quite different, but it was quite good, and he thought she would like it. By going this way, there would be a lot of camel riding and maybe sandstorms, and it would be *arduous*.

After all that explaining, he shrugged his shoulders, pulled on his few, long chin whiskers, and said, "If you don't have to go, why would you?"

Molly told him that she really wanted to go. She also told him about how Mister Tinker wanted to go to *the old country* but never did, and he regretted that he never did. Molly told him Mister Tinker died and never went.

Molly's feet are now warming up, and she feels cozy in bed. Maybe she is already asleep. It seems she can hear baby Charles crying and Momma going in to comfort him. But in any case, she is thinking about whether or not she should climb that Great Wall of China the wizard had told her about. That might be *arduous*.

Somewhere she hears a voice. Maybe it is the voice of the wizard, or maybe it is Mister Tinker's voice, or maybe it is her own, saying, "I know the heavens, and I can find my way home."

Postlude

Like fresh tulips in a vase.

At peak color, their petals unfold in the moment. Then, facing the light, almost in a dance, they twist and turn gracefully. As they inevitably age, they writhe, appearing to be struggling in agony. The color fades; the bloom withers, petals dry, and fall away.

Life is much like that—it's fleeting. Don't dally. Make the most of your moment.

Read, study, learn, work, hone your skills. Explore, experiment, play, understand materials, and create. Identify your talents. Apply yourself to solving problems.

Form good habits; you'll rely on them in old age.

Consider that every decision you make is a choice. If you make an error, rejoice, you've just learned something.

Trust your intuition; it is the grand fusion of all you know. It's an amalgam of information you and your mind's-eye observe, perceive, and collect from birth.

Live in appreciation for what you have, no matter how meager. Stay strong and as flexible as the bough of the tree to deal with what life brings.

If you have the means, travel. The source of your wisdom is bound up in your life experiences.

From time to time, pause, witness, reflect, and consider factors that define your generation.

Contribute. Give back. Be charitable.

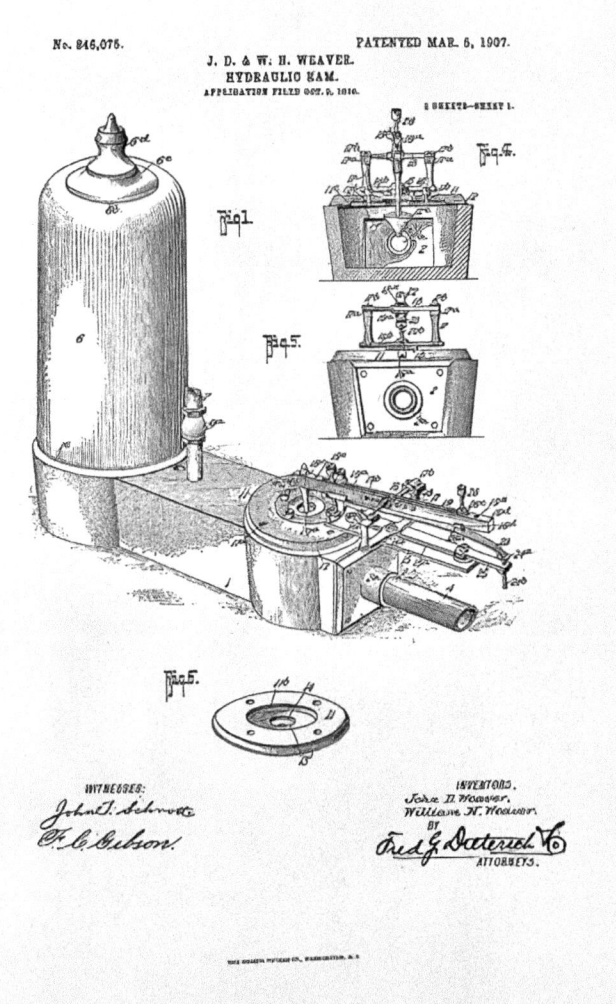

Hydraulic Ram Patent Image

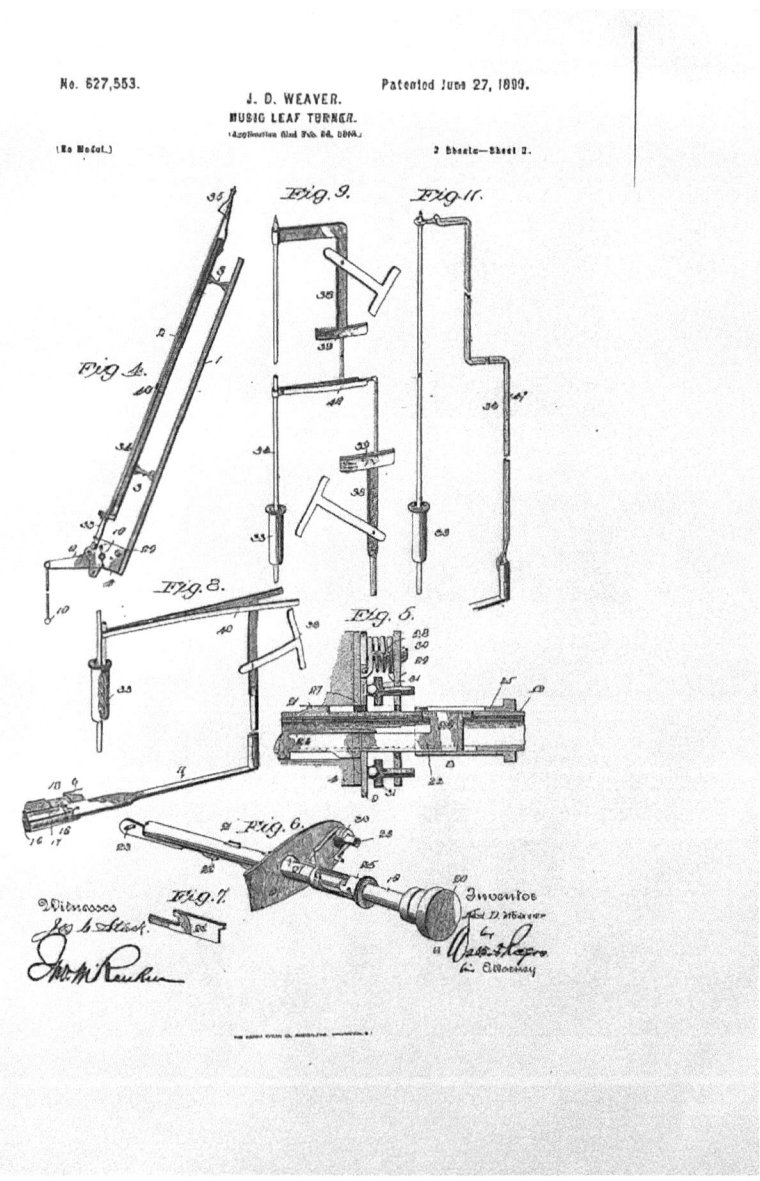

Music Leaf Turner Patent Image

Epilogue
John D. Weaver

There was such a man. His name is listed on the Pennsylvania Monument at Gettysburg National Cemetery, 11th Infantry, Company 1, Tab No. 2. He served in Co. E. 51st Regt, Pennsylvania Vol Infantry during the Civil War.

John D. Weaver was born in Pennsylvania. His father, John Henry Weaver, immigrated to the United States from Prussia in the 18th century; he was likely a clock maker. His mother was Anna Brown from Philadelphia. John married Sarah Jane Burke and, typical of that era, they had twelve children.

One of their children was my maternal grandmother, Esther Amelia, which makes John D. Weaver my great-grandfather. I never knew him. In fact, he died when my mother, Ann, was four years old, so she had little recollection of him.

As you might expect, not much is known of him—except what we gather from census and other existing records. So then, how did I come by his large, oak framed photographic portrait, and why has it been in the back of the closet in my guest room all these years? Was it there to motivate me to write this book? Maybe.

He enlisted at the age of eighteen years and fought in the Civil War. That he was disabled is recorded in his Pension Records. Some events in this book are taken from Affidavits for disability, which document him in the front lines at Petersburg, VA.

He was an inventor. Two patents, one for a hydraulic ram and one for a music leaf turner, are a matter of record in the US Patent Office. A large-framed portrait of him, a few family photographs, and a snapshot showing his daughter and son-in-law beside his automobile record his time; but that's about all we know—and there is no one left to ask.

The story of "Tinker" is loosely based on John D. Weaver's life. Some events and characters in this novel have been imagined. I've taken the liberty of using some family names for characters simply because I liked the name and for no other reason. However, the actions described, events, deeds, and thoughts are fictitious, conjured on my part, and supplanted from this period of early American history.

In the course of his lifespan, this country witnessed many remarkable changes; for example, the inventions of the automobile, indoor plumbing, the mechanization of farming, electrical power, and telephone lines beginning to lace communities together.

Yet, he began life carrying water, using oil lamps, an outhouse, and walking a long distance to and from school every day.

Though his life is wrapped in mystery and buried in time, fragments of information beg the question, what inspired him to create?

Surely he was inspired by Ford, Edison, Pullman, and others who all left their mark on his era, and eased living in that day and time and beyond? Inventing is born out of need. What inspired him to design a music leaf turner? His children did play the piano. Why a hydraulic ram? Did he see women and children carrying water to the cattle and think there might be a way to pump water to the fields? He was fascinated with cars, and he owned one, early on. He must have been a man with some means.

Years ago, I began recording oral family history. One day, my mother and I went in search of an aged relative I had never met. She was the daughter of Evangeline, John D. Weaver's sister. We found her Pennsylvania farmhouse surrounded by pristine, farmed fields, not far from the crossroads where Weaver's house once stood.

At first, his niece claimed no recollection of a John D. Weaver. I gently prodded her memory. Too many years had passed; she shook her head "no," as she struggled to make sense of what I said about him. When she was a small child, he would have been an elderly man. Finally, a smile came to her face, and she beamed. "Oh my, oh my, you're talking about Tinker, Tinker Weaver."

She told me he built a water wheel in the stream next to his house. It turned little figures in his parlor, to the delight of the children.

www.ingramcontent.com/pod-product-compliance
Lightning Source LLC
Chambersburg PA
CBHW042145170626
46815CB00006BA/308